Vampire plagues

LONDON

The screams were still loud outside, though Ben couldn't see where they came from. They were terrible, heart-rending, full of the knowledge of death. The shots had stopped.

The tents were pitched beneath some trees, to take advantage of the shade during the day. This early, the sun was just high enough for the trees to throw shadows. All the bats were out of their cages. Some were swarming around the site, staying within the shade. Others clustered together on the ground. They looked like writhing piles of black leaves. Then, horrified, Ben saw arms and legs protruding from the piles, and he realized where the screams were coming from. The bats were feeding on the porters. All of them!

Look out for…

Vampire plagues

LONDON

Sebastian Rook

SCHOLASTIC

For Joe Heaney

With special thanks to Ben Jeapes

Scholastic Children's Books
A division of Scholastic Ltd
Euston House, 24 Eversholt Street
London, NW1 1DB, UK
Registered office: Westfield Road, Southam, Warwickshire, CV47 0RA
SCHOLASTIC and associated logos are trademarks and or registered trademarks of
Scholastic Inc.

First published in the UK in 2004 by Scholastic Ltd, 2004
an imprint of Scholastic Inc.
Series created by Working Partners Ltd

This edition published in the UK by Scholastic Ltd, 2007

Copyright © Working Partners Ltd, 2004

10 digit ISBN 1 407 10628 7
13 digit ISBN 978 1407 10628 1

British Library Cataloguing-in-Publication Data
A CIP catalogue record for this book is available from the British Library

Printed in the UK by CPI Bookmarque, Croydon, CR0 4TD
Papers used by Scholastic Children's Books are made from wood grown in
sustainable forests.

1 3 5 7 9 10 8 6 4 2

www.scholastic.co.uk/zone

CHAPTER ONE

LONDON, MAY 1850

London's docks were alive with the bustle of a day's end. Ships crowded together, so many you could barely see the dark water between them, their masts a forest of tall, thin trees. Across the river, the Tower of London shone red in the light of the setting sun. The sailors and dockhands, busy about the boats, were painted red and black with stripes of sunset.

Jack Harkett lurked beside a pile of weathered tea crates from a Calcutta merchant ship. He was a thin and wiry boy, with dark brown hair and blue eyes. London's docks had been his home for all of his twelve years. He loved the exotic scents of spices from far-off places, the familiar smell of ship's tar and even the sour stench of the rank river mud when the tide was low. But, most of all, he loved the opportunities that the docks presented.

One such opportunity was heading his way now. A

gentleman in a frock coat and top hat was escorting a lady through the hustle and bustle of the dockside. The elegant couple picked their way through the crowd, around the crates and over the piles of horse dung. They clearly were not used to this place. Perhaps they were meeting someone, or maybe the man had an interest in a cargo somewhere.

Jack darted forward. "Meeting a ship, sir?" he asked, with a bright smile. "Show you where?"

The man looked Jack up and down and wrinkled his nose. The woman just glared at him. Neither had any time for shabby dockside urchins.

"I think not," the man replied stiffly. They walked off and the man pressed one hand against his hip pocket to check that his wallet was still there. Unfortunately, this simply served to show Jack exactly where the wallet was kept. He shrugged. He had tried the polite way – he always tried it first – but he had an empty stomach to fill, and if politeness didn't work, well, there were other ways. . .

Jack trailed the couple, drawing closer to them bit by bit. They were ten feet away when two youths cut in front of him, blocking the man from view. They were both much larger than Jack and he knew better than to interfere. They knew exactly what he was up to. One of them scowled hard at him to keep him away. The other brushed against the man and apologized. The gentleman nodded and kept walking with his lady. Jack caught a brief glimpse of the man's wallet disappearing into the youth's pocket. His face fell.

The youth who had been scowling at him grinned. "'Ere you are, squirt," he said, tossing Jack a penny. Then he and his partner in crime melted away into the crowd.

Jack snatched the penny from the air. It wasn't as much as he had hoped for, but it meant he could put something in his stomach. Everyone looked out for themselves around the docks, but nobody would let anyone else starve.

And that was pretty much how all of Jack's days went.

He spent the penny on a pie from a stall at the riverside. The sun was just a sliver on the horizon, now. Soon there would be no light to navigate, and those ships that hadn't quite made it to port would be dropping anchor in the river to wait for daylight. But one more was coming in, just catching the tide before it turned.

Jack sat on a bollard as he finished his pie and watched idly. It was a three-master, probably from India, America, or even Australia. Jack knew that London in the year 1850 was the heart of a vast empire that stretched around the world. He had lived all his life here, but his imagination loved to roam. One day, he promised himself, he would visit these exotic places himself.

The ship reached the dockside just as the sun finally vanished. Suddenly a great black cloud seemed to billow up from the deck. But it wasn't smoke or fog. It was something else – something animal. It swooped straight at Jack and he fell backwards off the bollard with a yell. Black creatures, large as crows, swarmed only feet overhead. They were bats, hundreds of them, the largest he had ever seen. For a moment the dark, seething mass hovered in the night sky. Then the bats peeled off in every direction, vanishing down the alleys and lanes of the docks. Some of them dispersed across the river, flying towards the Tower and the mighty dome of St Paul's.

Jack watched them go, then turned wonderingly back to the ship. Surely it had come from some uncharted continent, some far-off island jungle. Great explorers must have penetrated to the dark interior of a hostile land and brought back extraordinary, outlandish creatures. And possibly strange treasures! Jack rubbed his hands together in the chilly night air and made his way over to where the ship was docking.

Now that the sun was gone, the ship was just a hulking shape in the gloom, barely lit by the shoreside lanterns. Dockers stood on the quay, ready to take the lines as it drew alongside.

Jack loitered in the shadows of a warehouse and watched. He knew better than to let himself be seen. Incoming ships were easy targets, and the dockers would probably chase him off if they saw him.

The harbour master paced up and down on the quayside as the dockers made the ship fast. At this time of day he should have been on his way home. He wouldn't have been expecting another ship to come in. The gangplank came down – a wooden bridge up into the darkness of the deck. The harbour master and the shore crew hurried on board. Jack made himself comfortable. He knew there would be forms to fill out and customs procedures to go through. It would take a while, but eventually he would be able to sneak on board and explore.

But, in less than a minute, there were shouts of surprise in the darkness and the men came hurrying back down the gangplank. They had the purposeful look of people wanting to run but trying hard not to. Jack heard someone mutter "Ain't natural" as he hurried by.

Jack stared at them as they hastened away in the gloom. Then he looked back at the ship. It sat by the quayside, a still, silent shape.

Too still, too silent.

There was no sound of sailors calling to one another. No footsteps echoing on the wooden decks and, strangest of all, no hurry to unload the cargo.

Jack frowned and took a step forward, then stopped as another figure appeared at the top of the gangplank. This was no sailor, no dockhand. It was a broad, heavy man; a gentleman, judging by his dress. He wore a long black coat with a fur collar and a polished, black stovepipe hat. In one hand he carried a silver-topped cane. He looked as if he had just come from the theatre in the West End, not the other side of the world. He paused for a moment to adjust his cravat, then set off down the gangplank, swinging his cane. He walked right past Jack and into the night. The shadows of the docks swallowed him up, as though welcoming him home.

Jack shivered. He didn't know why. This wasn't the first ship to dock at night in London. The man was not the first well-dressed gent to come ashore. But something here was *wrong*. The docks were usually full of life and energy, even after dark, but something about this ship just seemed to have sucked the energy away.

Jack took a deep breath. He had set himself the challenge of going on board the ship, and that was what he would do. If his nerve failed him, he would never survive in London. He slipped from the shadows, but another movement at the top of the gangplank sent him scurrying back to his hiding place.

A boy stepped out into the light from the shore and edged hesitantly down to the dockside.

Jack let out a sigh of relief. The boy could not have been much older than Jack himself. Unlike the man, he really did look as if he had been on a voyage. He was thin, his fair hair was tangled and matted, and his clothes were grimy and rumpled like Jack's own. Jack guessed he was a cabin boy or a sailor's son. Whoever he was, Jack felt much more inclined to talk to him than to the man in black.

Jack let him approach, then stepped out from his hiding place. "Evening," he said cheerily.

To Jack's surprise, the boy stared at him in horror for a second, then fled.

"Hey!" Jack called. He threw up his hands in disgust and turned back to the ship. Then he thought again. Someone or something on that ship had scared off the harbour master and dockers. Whatever it was, it surely couldn't have been that boy – and it might still be on board. Jack had no desire to tangle with someone, or some*thing*, that could see off a gang of dockers – but another boy he could handle. He turned again and began to give chase.

The other boy had a strange, shambling run, as if his legs were seized up through disuse. Jack's longer legs quickly ate up the distance between them. The boy had reached the deep, dark lane between two brick warehouses which rose up on either side. This part of the docks was used only for storage and there was no one else around. Occasional lanterns dispersed the gloom and as the boy approached each light, his shadow would swell and dance, looking like a giant on the sheer brick walls. Then it shrank again as he ran on past.

The boy stopped for a moment and bent over with his hands on his knees, drawing deep breaths. He looked up, saw Jack approaching and pelted away again, down a side alley. Jack scowled, then grinned and slowed to a casual walk. He waited at the entrance to the alley, with his arms folded.

The boy had already discovered it was a dead end. He

stood with his back pressed to the wall and stared at Jack. "You won't have me!" he said. His voice had a faint tremor in it, as if he was putting every ounce of energy into sounding brave. "You won't have me!"

"That's as well, 'cos I don't want you," Jack retorted. "What was you thinking, taking off like that?"

"I had to get away," the boy mumbled. He was like a trapped animal, glancing up and down and around, all the while looking for a way out. Only half his mind was on what he was saying. "Had to get away . . . been there so long. . ."

"You're touched in the head," Jack said sadly.

This close, he could see he had been wrong about who the boy was. The clothes were ragged, but under the dirt Jack could see what had once been a smart flannel suit. And his voice was cultured. At any other time, Jack would have thought him a toff and had nothing more to do with him. But now his instincts as a dock dweller were taking over. It was the same instinct that had made the older boy throw him a penny earlier on. You looked after other unfortunates like yourself.

"Maybe I should take you back," he began.

"*No!*" the boy screamed. His eyes were wide and his mouth gaped.

Jack recognized real terror. "Bully you, did he?" he asked quietly. "That fancy gent in the black coat?"

"Bully me?" The boy's voice was bitter. "No. He never found me. I was too clever."

"Well, good on you." Jack studied the boy. He couldn't just leave him here. "Well, if you're not going back to the boat. . ."

"B-Bedford Square." The boy drew himself up. "I need to get to Bedford Square urgently. That's where I live. Can you show me the way?"

"That up west, then?" Jack asked.

"Bloomsbury." The boy pronounced it *Bloomsbr'eh*.

"I see." Bloomsbury was off his usual patch, but Jack knew how to find it. He scratched his head. If someone in a place like that was interested in this boy, there might even be a reward in it for him. "Bloomsbury it is. Come on, we'll go and –"

The boy's knees began to fold. Jack caught him just in time and gently set him back on his feet. He was as light as a feather and, under the remains of the coat, Jack could feel his ribs.

"You're famished, aren't you?" Jack remarked.

The boy nodded weakly. "I haven't had much to eat . . . had to eat what I could . . . for weeks. . ."

"Then that's the first thing we'll change. You come with me and tell me all about it." Jack led the boy out of the alley. "You got a name?" he asked.

"Benedict Cole." The boy smiled weakly. "Ben to my friends."

"I'm Jack – to everyone as knows me," Jack replied.

He was careful to walk slowly. He didn't want Ben to collapse again.

"I don't like these alleys," Ben commented. His eyes darted up into the dark. "Not enough light."

"Don't you worry about the dark," Jack told him. "I been around long enough to look after us both."

"You haven't seen what I've seen," Ben said, with such finality and gloom that Jack gave up trying to cheer him.

The hubbub of a crowded public house could be heard ahead. As they turned the next corner, the friendly flicker of gaslights beckoned to them.

Ben's pace quickened. And then they were in the thick of it – caught up in the usual jostle of dockworkers in the evening, coming and going to the pub, laughing and chatting. After the echoing silence of the warehouses it was a welcome return to warmth and humanity.

"Feeling better?" Jack asked Ben.

Ben nodded. "And I'm looking forward to that food," he replied, with a shy eagerness.

"I bet you are," Jack grinned. "And no more dark, eh?"

"Oh, they can still see you." Ben, who for just a moment had sounded like a normal boy looking forward to a meal, once again sounded terrified. "When it's night, they can always see you. Look!" He clutched at Jack's arm and pointed upwards. Jack followed his finger. He was looking at the moon – and a small black shape that flitted across it.

"Just a bat," Jack said carelessly.

Ben stared up for a few heartbeats more. Then, slowly, he relaxed. "Yes," he said. "I imagine so."

"Not like those ones that came off the boat," Jack added. "Huge great things, they were."

Ben groaned. "Oh, no. They're awake? They're in London?"

"Didn't you see 'em?"

"I was too busy hiding from them. No, I . . . I didn't see them wake up." Ben looked close to tears. "I was hoping I could . . . before they. . . Oh, never mind."

"Hoping you could do what?" asked Jack curiously.

"I was hoping I could warn someone. Do something," Ben replied. "But it's too late now."

"So what's wrong with 'em?" Jack queried. "They got a disease or something?"

Ben looked at him oddly. "A disease?" he repeated absently. "Yes. You could say that. . ."

The Admiral Nelson was a cheerful riverside inn. Loud bursts of laughter and snatches of singing spilled out into the cool night air. Nelson himself, one-eyed and one-armed, immaculate in his admiral's uniform, looked down from the painted sign that swung over the door.

Ben hesitated as they approached. "It looks very, um . . . crowded," he said.

"We're not going *in*," Jack said. "Going in takes money, which I'm guessing you don't have."

"I'm afraid you're right." Suddenly Ben's eyebrows shot up. "Are you going to *steal* food?"

Jack had to laugh. "Not if I know what's good for me. Come on."

He led Ben round to the back of the inn, secretly pleased about the state of Ben's clothes. Had they been clean and smart, such a well-dressed lad would have stood out a mile.

A large, round woman had come out of the back door with a tray of scraps, which she flung on to the rubbish heap.

Jack nudged Ben. "Look small," he said. "Big eyes. Like this." He widened his eyes, bit his lip and imagined himself to be even scrawnier than his companion. Then he called, "Evening, Molly!"

The woman jumped. "Why, look who it is. Out here on the rat heap, the cheekiest rat of them all. How are you, Jack?"

Jack put on his best smile. This was all part of the ritual. Molly was just one of the many women who had cared for him when he was little. It was the closest he came to any kind of family. "I was wondering. . ." he began.

"Well, do us a favour and wonder somewheres else, then," Molly retorted. "I'm busy and. . . Hello! Who's this?"

Ben had come out of the shadows. Jack was pleased to see the boy following his advice and looking pitiable, until he realized that that was just how Ben looked naturally – absolutely famished.

"This is—" Jack began.

"A young lad at death's door!" Molly exclaimed. "You

two wait here." She went back in, and reappeared a moment later with a couple of bundles. "Bit of bread, pie, some potatoes. Best I can do before Bill notices and docks me pay."

Jack grinned, and Ben stared at the bundles as if they had come down from heaven.

"Thanks, Molly. Be seeing you," Jack said. He put a friendly hand on Ben's shoulder and led him away.

They found a quiet courtyard, where they sat on a low wall and Ben tore his bundle open. He picked up the hunk of bread and buried his face in it, his jaw working to get it all down.

Jack had to pull it gently away from him. "Oi, not so fast. I seen people eat after being starving. They wolfs it down and then they brings it all back up again. Easy does it."

It was easier for Jack – the pie he had bought earlier was still warm inside him. He fed the meal to Ben bit by bit, letting the boy take it in slowly, giving his stomach time to adjust to having food in it once again. At one point Ben sniffled and Jack realized that the other boy was crying softly. "What is it?" he asked gently.

"It . . . it's nothing." For a moment Ben looked furious that Jack had seen him crying. He took a bite out of a potato. "It's so good to be home and to be eating." He gave a bashful smile. "Thank you for all your help. You know, I haven't always been a starving stowaway."

"I guessed that," Jack said. It was the first time Ben

had mentioned being a stowaway at all, but Jack had guessed that, too. "What got you from Bedford Square to here?"

Ben sighed. "Have you heard of Harrison Cole?"

Jack shook his head.

"Harrison Cole is an anthropologist. He studies peoples and cultures – especially ancient civilizations. And he's . . . he was my father," Ben explained.

Jack nodded and remained quiet to let Ben talk. Unfortunately, Ben seemed to have dried up. The boy stared down at the cobblestones for so long that Jack began to feel uncomfortable. He drew breath to say something, but suddenly Ben began to speak again.

"And his partner, Edwin Sherwood, was an archaeologist. He was always looking for ancient cities. They're famous – Cole and Sherwood. They were old friends and they always travelled together. With Sir Donald Finlay." His tone grew dark once more. "You've seen Sir Donald."

"The man in the coat?"

"The same," Ben agreed.

"Is he another antelope-a-list?" inquired Jack.

"Anthropologist? No, he's a biologist. He studied animals," Ben explained. "The three of them worked together for years," he continued. "They've been all over the world, exploring and investigating, finding new things. As soon as Emily and I were old enough, we went with them."

"Who's Emily?" asked Jack.

Ben blinked, as if surprised he had left out that detail. "Emily is my sister. She's a year older than me. She'll be here in London now, I expect. She came down with a fever just as we were about to leave on our last journey, and so she had to stay behind. She was frightfully disappointed, but our housekeeper will have looked after her. I promised to keep a journal so that she could read it when we got back."

He patted his pocket, and pulled out a battered, cardboard-bound notebook. "It has a lot more in it than she expected," he said thoughtfully.

Jack was reminded of his ambitions for travelling the world. This rich boy and his sister had already done it – and they hadn't even had to ask. "Good of your old man to take you," he commented, wistfully.

"Our mother died when we were very little," Ben explained. "Father could never bear to leave us behind. Anyway, our latest expedition was to Mexico. We left in January." He lapsed into silence again.

"Did you find anything?" Jack prompted.

"Oh, yes."

Another silence.

"What was it?" Jack asked after a moment.

Ben turned his head slowly to look at Jack with tormented eyes. "Hell!" he whispered.

CHAPTER TWO

FIVE MONTHS EARLIER. . .

From the journal of Benedict Cole
30th January 1850

Mexico in sight!

After four weeks in a world two hundred feet long and fifty feet wide, Emily, I am looking forward to a change. I have explored every inch of our noble vessel, from stem to stern and from the bottom of the hold to the tops of the masts (two hundred feet above the wave tops, swaying gently from side to side!). And I can safely say it holds no new wonders for me.

Ah, but Mexico. . .

We have sailed across the Atlantic, through the chain of the Bahamas and the Straits of Florida, and down the Yucatan Channel between Mexico and Cuba. And now, the coast of the Yucatan peninsula has come into view, low on the horizon. The Yucatan sticks out from the bottom of Mexico into the Caribbean like a big thumb. According to the books, the entire peninsula – 200 miles across and 300 miles from end to end – is one flat limestone shelf, only a few dozen feet above sea level and with very little in the way of hills or mountains. The east coast, where we will put into port, is edged with low bluffs of white stone, indented with bays. There is more vegetation here than on the low and sandy north and west coasts. The dry season lasts from October until May, so we are not expecting rain.

We are heading for Puerto Morelos and the captain says—

The wind shifted abruptly and blew the pages of Ben's journal over. He looked up. He had been sitting with his back to the main-mast, letting the breeze ruffle his hair and keep the open pages of his book flat. Now the ship had heeled, turning into the wind. The wide, blue sky seemed to wheel above him. The wind blowing into Ben's face tasted of salt and land. Sailors ran past him and climbed nimbly up the rigging. Others, in teams down on the deck, heaved on lines, while up above, the flapping sails were hauled in and tied to their booms.

Ben closed the book and stood up. He stretched and crossed the deck to a group of men standing by the rail. "What's happening?" he asked.

His father turned. He was a tall, thin man with dark, receding hair and a warm smile. "A pilot's coming out to guide us into port," he explained.

"Over there," said Harrison's companion, pointing to a small boat which was approaching rapidly. Edwin Sherwood was shorter than his friend and colleague, but his smile was no less warm as he looked at Ben. Ben couldn't remember a time when he hadn't known his godfather, whom he called Uncle Edwin. Harrison and Edwin had been friends at Oxford and partners in exploration all Ben's life, though Edwin's own field was archaeology.

Ben watched the pilot's boat bouncing gaily over the blue waves towards them. It was a long, narrow cutter with a single triangular sail.

There was a stiff breeze coming off the shore, for which Ben was very grateful. The sun was hot, and the breeze was the only thing that made his Norfolk jacket and tie – which he was expected to wear constantly in public, and most of the time in private – bearable.

"Let go the anchor!" shouted one of the sailors.

The anchor plunged down into the sea, its cable running out behind it with a whir. Ben looked down at the grating beneath his feet. He was standing over the cable locker, a damp dark place where the several hundred feet of anchor-cable were coiled and stored.

Ben glanced up as he felt someone tousle his hair.

"And how's our expedition diarist?" inquired Sir Donald. He was a bluff man, broad across the shoulders and fair-haired with a drooping moustache.

Ben smiled, but politely moved his head away. He wished Sir Donald wouldn't do that, though he knew it was a sign of affection.

Sir Donald didn't give Ben time to answer the question. "Looking forward to landing, eh?" he added.

"Oh, yes, sir," Ben replied eagerly. "Very much."

The cutter drew alongside and the pilot expertly jumped for the ship's ladder. The smaller boat pulled away as the pilot clambered up on to the ship's deck. Five minutes later the sails were unfurled again and the anchor was hauled up. The ship got under way once more, heading into the port of Puerto Morelos for the last mile of its long journey.

Standing at the rail, watching Mexico approach, Ben Cole had never felt safer or happier.

From the journal of Benedict Cole
30th January 1850 (continued)

Despite its grand name, Puerto Morelos is more like a sleepy fishing village than a bustling port. But it's convenient for the interior of the peninsula, which is why Sir Donald chose it as a destination. Ours is the largest ship moored at the long dock that extends out to sea, though there are a handful of smaller fishing craft.

Standing on solid ground again felt very strange after the constant rocking of the ship and the sun was painfully bright. Every building is covered in white plaster to reflect the heat; you soon learn to wear a hat with a brim that shades your face, or walk about with your eyes half-closed against the glare.

The sun affects the whole way of life here. The dock-workers dress in baggy, off-white cotton slacks and wide hats. No one moves about at speed. And the sun bakes everything dry.

We are spending our first night ashore in a cockroach-ridden hotel facing into the zocolo – the town square – which is at the end of the fishing dock. I'm sitting on the balcony as I write this. The zocolo is a tree-shaded park, a gathering place at day's end. The night air is warm, and it carries the fragrant scents of the forests and the sizzling, spicy smells of food being cooked in the street below. Someone in another room is playing a guitar and singing about a lost love.

All our crates are unloaded from the ship and tomorrow Sir Donald will recruit some locals to act as porters. Then we will set off into the interior. The adventure is beginning, Emily! How I wish you could see it.

The land beyond Puerto Morelos was dry and flat. There was no running water wider than a stream in the Yucatan: with no mountains to feed them, rivers did not exist. Fresh water came up through cenotes, holes in the limestone floor of the peninsula. They tapped into vast, natural underground reservoirs that were fed during the rainy season.

The party headed south-west from the port. They rode in a procession of ox-drawn carts along a rutted track. Ben, his father, Edwin Sherwood and Sir Donald rode in the lead cart. Behind them came a pair of carts stacked with empty crates, and riding these, or walking alongside, were the forty native porters Sir Donald had recruited. The majority were Spanish settlers but a small minority were pure Mayan, descendants of the people whose great empire had once dominated the Yucatan. They were short and stocky, with straight black hair and flat faces. Their leader, Miguel, was the son of a Spanish colonist and a Mayan.

"We know so little about the Mayans," said Harrison Cole as they travelled. "Their ancestors were probably here before the time of Christ. As far as we can tell, their empire fell about a thousand years ago. Then a new people came along, the, um. . ."

"Toltecs," put in Uncle Edwin from Ben's other side. "We think they sailed across the Gulf of Mexico. Their leader was a chap called Quetzalcóatl. According to legend he will one day return from the direction of the rising sun. That legend made it rather easy for the Spanish conquerors when they came from that direction in the sixteenth century. Anyway, by then the Mayans and Toltecs had combined into a new society.

21

It wasn't as powerful as the classical Mayan Empire, but it was enough to give the Spanish a headache. And these chaps –" he waved a hand at some of the porters – "are their descendants. They have a proud heritage."

"Of human sacrifice among other things," said Ben's father, with a grim smile.

Uncle Edwin shrugged. "Indeed. But this is an inhospitable land, Harry. Anyone who can make a living here, let alone carve out an empire, has my respect."

Ben was silent, considering the Ancient Mayan civilization and its tradition of human sacrifice. He wondered about the other ways in which that ancient culture would have differed from his own – and thought that people would not have had to wear jackets and ties for a start!

The road curved back to the north and Sir Donald decided that they would have to leave the track and walk. Their destination lay ahead, in the jungles of the Yucatan heartland. The porters carried the crates and the expedition's supplies and the party set off, away from the track, through brittle, knee-high scrub. Gradually the dry and thorny forest wrapped itself around them. The air became warmer and more humid and the trees grew taller, bit by bit closing out the sunlight. Ben realized, with a thrill of excitement, that they were entering the jungle.

* * *

From the journal of Benedict Cole
14th February 1850

I have been two weeks in the jungle! It feels much longer.
But how shall I describe it to you, Emily? Where should
I begin?

Think of a church. Now imagine the air inside it to be
very, very hot and heavy and humid. The windows and
the floor are covered with rotting leaves, so there is a
stench of decaying vegetation and no light. (Even at
midday, we sometimes have to light a lamp.) Imagine the
pillars are trees, not in two neat rows down the aisle but
everywhere. And they are thickly wrapped in vines and
ivy and every kind of climbing plant, because everything
wants to get up above the tree canopy and reach the
sunlight. You are beginning to get a feel for the Yucatan
jungle.

Father, Uncle Edwin and Sir Donald are in excellent
spirits. Sir Donald doesn't mind stopping to let Father
and Uncle Edwin climb over ruined temples and crawl
down hidden passageways. And we're all delighted when
Sir Donald spots a new kind of bird or creature.

The wildlife is brightly coloured and quite spectacular.
I've seen a spider with a yellow body and legs, and black
knees. It's very poisonous, apparently. I've seen swallow-
tailed butterflies: their wings are less brightly black and
yellow, but the tips fan out into a fantastic spectrum
of colours. And not everything crawls. You should see

the birds! Toucans with gleaming red beaks. And
hummingbirds, which are delicate little wisps of shiny blue.
We pitched camp a few hours ago. . .

"Why here?" Ben asked. He glanced around. They had found a small clearing and the tents were being set up around it. He and his father shared one; Uncle Edwin and Sir Donald shared another. The porters preferred to sleep out in the open, and they were already dropping their bedrolls around the edge of the clearing.

Edwin Sherwood looked up from his map and grinned. "Why here, Ben?" he said. "Come with me. I've got something to show you."

Ben walked over to him. Uncle Edwin stood behind him and put his hands on Ben's shoulders. He turned Ben in a slow half circle. "Apart from the tents and the porters, what do you see?" he asked.

Ben shrugged. "Trees," he replied. "I think there's some kind of parrot up there. That tree trunk might have a snake in it, so we'll have to beat it out before we sit down. . ." He felt pleased with himself for remembering that particular bit of jungle lore.

"Apart from the wildlife, as well," Uncle Edwin said.

Ben looked carefully. Then he sighed. "Nothing," he answered. "What do you see?"

"Well. . ." Uncle Edwin crouched down beside him and pointed. "I see that."

Ben peered in the direction his godfather was

indicating. Through the undergrowth, a dark mass rose out of the ground. "It's a hill," said Ben.

"A hill? In dull, flat Yucatan? Come here."

Uncle Edwin led Ben through the trees to the foot of the hill. It did rise out of the ground very steeply, but it was so densely covered with undergrowth that Ben saw no reason to change his mind.

But then Uncle Edwin pulled out his knife and swung it at the vegetation. After two or three precise strokes it clanked against stone. Uncle Edwin scraped the blade along the slope and more stone appeared. Then Ben gasped. A square, ugly face was glaring at him out of the stonework.

"Give me a hand, Ben?" Uncle Edwin said, but Ben was already running back to the camp to get a knife of his own.

They worked together for an hour, by which time they had uncovered some thirty or forty square feet of stone. Meanwhile, Ben's eyes were making out the rest of the detail.

They had found what seemed to be the bottom steps of a broad staircase. It rose up and up, to a point far above them, and shell carvings were set into the stonework.

"What is it?" Ben asked breathlessly as they walked slowly back to the camp.

"If it follows the typical pattern, it will be a pyramid," Uncle Edwin replied. He glanced back. "A very big pyramid, probably with a temple on the top."

"Were you looking for it?"

"Oh, I had my suspicions. I was in Mexico five years ago. There's a large city about fifty miles from here, to the west. That's where I found the bat."

Ben nodded. Even though he had been a little boy at the time, he remembered the excitement when Uncle Edwin returned to England with his treasure: a bat-shaped gold statuette. It had made his name as an archaeologist, and was now on display in the British Museum.

"We know there is a network of *sacbeobs* running through the jungle," Edwin continued, "that is, avenues through the jungle, which are lined with stones – massive stones, six feet high. We've found bits and pieces of them here and there, and they seem to converge at a point somewhere in this region. I think this city may be that point."

"So there'll be more than a pyramid," Ben said eagerly.

"Oh, much more," Uncle Edwin agreed. "Temples. Houses. Halls. And this, if I'm not very much mistaken, is a ball court."

"This" was the clearing where the tents stood, but now Ben's eyes had grown used to discerning hidden things. He studied the ground carefully, and the surrounding undergrowth. The clearing was long, more like a rectangle than a circle, and the ground was flat and hard. Now that he looked, he could make out low, sloping stone terraces, running the length of the clearing on either side. The camp was pitched between them.

"A ball court?" he repeated in amazement.

"Oh, they had their uses," Uncle Edwin told him with a twinkle in his eye. "But explaining that can be Harry's job."

Harrison Cole was delighted at the discovery. He and Ben worked away at one of the terraces while Edwin returned to the pyramid. The terrace started near the ground on one side and rose to about shoulder height on the other. It had been a smooth, paved surface before the jungle got to it. Near the top, Ben's father used his knife to hack away a small bush, revealing a stone hoop set into the wall.

"Mayan ball games had a ritual purpose," he explained as they worked. "The contest between the teams represented the battle between life and death. The floor of the court symbolized the earth's surface, and the ball wasn't allowed to touch it. The ball is thought to have been made of rubber, so it bounced off the walls of the court and off the players themselves. The captain of the losing team was sacrificed – probably by decapitation."

"*What?*" Ben cried, aghast.

His father smiled. "Fate, Ben. Obviously, the gods had chosen the loser to die. It gave the players some incentive, that's for sure."

"Decapitated," Ben murmured in horror.

Harrison still smiled, but his eyes were serious. "They were not a pleasant people, Ben, remember that. At the very best, you were expected to sacrifice your own blood to the gods. People would pierce their tongues, or lips. They would walk around with thorns stuck into them, keeping the wounds open so that the blood continued to flow. And at the very worst, people were sacrificed. Would you believe it used to be a privilege? Only kings and royalty were eligible for sacrifice at first. Eventually, you could buy orphans, just so the priest could lay them on an altar and cut out their beating hearts." Harrison Cole sighed. "In some ways it's a shame we will never see the Mayan Empire at its height, but let's not mourn its passing either, eh?"

From the journal of Benedict Cole
16th February 1850

Father is right, of course, Emily. It's a strange feeling, to stand in a temple and to know that once people were sacrificed there. We can only be thankful that the Ancient Mayan gods are dead and gone.

We have continued exploring the city, although our little expedition will never uncover more than a fraction of this place. Uncle Edwin suspects it covers several square miles, like the other city where he found the golden bat.

In the buildings here there are no arches, nothing is

rounded. To make an opening in a wall, like a door, the best the engineers could do was to lie a single stone slab across two supports. That means no door or window could be more than a few feet wide. Everything we have seen (apart from the pyramids, which are just piles of stone) was built low. They didn't have bricks, just stone, so if they built too high the buildings would collapse under their own weight.

It sounds limited, yet within those limitations the Mayans produced great cities in this inhospitable place — ones that would rival ancient Rome. Like Uncle Edwin, I admire their accomplishments, if not their ways.

But, where did they all go? The city is well preserved, apart from the jungle growth. There is no sign that it fell in a war. A plague? Well, perhaps, but then where are the skeletons?

Uncle Edwin says that these are questions asked of all the Mayan cities. The first great Mayan civilization fell in the ninth or tenth centuries, before the Toltecs came. Almost overnight, the cities were abandoned. Perhaps we will never know why.

Uncle Edwin is determined to find out, though. He says this city will make his reputation once and for all when he returns home. He expects to come back here next year with an expedition five times the size of this one, and he says (Father permitting) we can come too! I know you will love it, Emily. This place will fascinate you.

This is our last night here. Sir Donald has been patient

with the enthusiasms of Father and Uncle Edwin, but he is a biologist first and foremost. He still wants to head yet further into the interior in search of new species, and tomorrow we set off.

CHAPTER THREE

From the journal of Benedict Cole
6th March 1850

Well, the city is now behind us. We are deep in the jungle and Sir Donald is delighted with what we have found here.

We have filled about half the crates we brought from Puerto Morelos. Sir Donald is determined to bring home alive as many of these creatures as he can. He says several of them aren't yet known to science. I can't even write their names down for you, because we don't yet know what their names are going to be!

Let's see. So far we have five different types of rodent, ranging from something that looks like a rat and eats our leftovers, to a little vole the size of my thumb that has to be fed leaves four or five times a day. We also have a colourful collection of birds — parrots, toucans, and my favourite, which is a pretty little thing the size of a finch, *with a green back, blue head and yellow chest. Its name, and Sir Donald swears he isn't making this up, is the violaceous trogon. Or, if you prefer its Latin name, Trogon violaceus. With a name like that, it would be my favourite even if it was as ugly as a brick.*

And we have a number of tree creatures. Squirrels, fuller bodied than the English type, and grey with it. Lemurs the size of your hand with huge eyes for seeing in the gloom. And a gorgeous monkey with fur that gleams like beaten gold. Of course, we can only keep herbivores. We could capture carnivores too, but what would they eat, apart from the rest of the collection?

I've mentioned feeding so much because that is my job. It's quite a responsibility and I was very proud when Sir Donald chose me for it. I have to be up before the rest of the camp – not because early rising is as good for you as Father says it is (I'm sure it isn't), but because the jungle's oven heat is just about bearable early in the day.

Ben looked up as the tent flap was pulled open.

Harrison Cole stuck his head in and smiled. "Miguel's going hunting, Ben. Fancy going with him?" he asked.

Ben was torn between finishing his report for Emily and the chance of some activity – but only briefly. He quickly jumped up, straightened his tie and hurried outside.

They had pitched camp in another clearing, this time a natural one, and it followed the usual pattern of all their camps. The tents were side by side, and the stack of crates sat opposite them across the clearing. In between were the cooking fire, the porters' bedrolls, and a couple of trestle tables on which to work. Edwin Sherwood sat at one of these now, going over notes he had made back at the ancient city.

Sir Donald was in the middle of the clearing, talking to Miguel, the head porter, who had a quiver full of arrows slung over one shoulder and a bow in his left hand. Harrison waved Ben over to Miguel and then joined Edwin to help with the notes.

Miguel grinned at Ben as he peered down at him from beneath the brim of his battered leather hat. "We go hunting food, *sí*? For dinner?"

"*Sí!*" Ben agreed. "What are we hunting?"

Miguel tapped his nose. "Who knows? We will soon see."

They waved goodbye to the others, and headed into the bush. Rather to his disappointment, Ben didn't get to carry a bow and arrow. That was Miguel's preserve. Ben suspected he had been brought along as a ploy to keep him occupied, rather than to make a serious contribution with his hunting skills, but he didn't mind. There was something exciting about hunting in the wilds of the Yucatan jungle.

Miguel was moving down a faint trail through the undergrowth, walking slightly crouched. His eyes were fixed on the ground. Ben followed hopefully. Almost immediately the jungle had swallowed them up. They were out of sight and sound of the camp now, surrounded by the smells and animal calls of the rainforest.

Miguel stopped suddenly and pointed. "See?" he demanded.

Ben saw a trail of small footprints. In the few areas of bare earth, they looked almost like bird steps – three thin, pointed toes set like an arrowhead.

Ben looked blank. Miguel clicked his tongue and held his pointed fingers up to his head, to indicate horns. "*Es un ciervo pequeño*," he said. "Deer."

"Deer!" Ben repeated. He suddenly felt hungry.

Miguel slid silently off the trail like a snake into the undergrowth. Ben tried to follow him but thorns snagged on his jacket. He tugged and the jacket came free, but the thorny branch snapped back to where it had been with a crack. Miguel shot him an angry glance. Ben bit his tongue just in time to stop himself apologizing – he suspected even a whisper would be too loud.

Ben had no idea how Miguel tracked the deer. He couldn't see any sign of the hoofprints at all. Yet for a good half hour they moved at a slow crouch through the jungle. Perhaps it was Miguel's Mayan blood that put him in tune with the hot, humid forest, but somehow his practised eyes could follow the deer's progress through the undergrowth: here it had bent a leaf, there it had brushed a twig. Every now and then Miguel would pause and study something more closely: a tuft of hair on a spiny plant, some fresh droppings in the mulch.

The heat was stifling. Sweat ran down Ben's forehead and trickled down his back. And then the most unlikely scent reached his nostrils. It was almost . . . *rosy*. He breathed in deeply, and gagged. It was as if his nose and mouth were suddenly blocked. There was indeed something rosy nearby, but its fragrance was so strong it was cloying, almost nauseating. It seemed to fill the air with a choking syrup. Ben wrinkled his nose and willed the irritation away.

Miguel stopped. He was suddenly rigid as a statue. Ben took the hint and tried to stay as still as he could. It wasn't easy because he was leaning over, his knees bent in mid-step. Soon he could feel his thighs aching with the challenge.

Staring dead ahead, Miguel brought up his bow and arrow. Ben followed the shaft of the arrow with his eyes and drew an imaginary line from the tip into the undergrowth.

Finally, he saw the deer. It stood against what looked like a sheer, green wall that was studded with red flowers, and it blended into the shadows almost perfectly. The small animal was no more than two feet tall at the shoulder and it was grazing innocently on something at the foot of the wall.

Miguel took aim and drew back the bowstring.

But the rosy smell was too strong for Ben. The

fragrance tickled his nostrils and irritated his sinuses. His eyes started to water. He couldn't help it. He sneezed.

The deer shot off just as Miguel let the arrow fly. Ben stared in horror at the place where the creature had been. The deer just seemed to have vanished.

Miguel turned and glared at Ben. He cursed in Spanish and straightened up – there was no point in hiding now.

"Gone!" Miguel said angrily. He stalked through the brush to the foot of the green wall. "Now we never find it again. See?" He pointed. "There it go."

Ben came forward out of curiosity. Now he could see that the green wall was a thick row of rose bushes. The leaves were dark and packed tightly together. The flowers were a rich, blood red, and gave off the overpowering scent that had made Ben sneeze.

Miguel was pointing at a small hole in the bushes. It was just large enough to take a small deer. The thorns would make it very hard for anything larger.

Ben wondered how sharp they were. Perhaps Miguel was just being pessimistic. He reached out and touched a thorn, then hissed and snatched his hand back. The thorns were cruel and curved like fangs. He had barely touched one and yet it had sliced through his skin with ease. Deep red blood was welling up from the cut. He put his injured finger in his mouth and sighed. No one was going to be able to crawl through that hole: not a man, not even a twelve-year-old boy. They would be cut to pieces.

Miguel snorted, a grim kind of chuckle. "*La rosa de la sangre*," he said, and even Ben with his minimal Spanish understood *rose of blood*. Or blood rose.

"Do you know it?" he asked.

Miguel shrugged. "*Sí*. A weed. Much of it in this area." He stepped back and looked at the thicket thoughtfully. "But I've never seen this much before."

He turned and walked straight back to the camp without a pause. Ben swallowed his shame at losing dinner and followed.

Within the hour, to Ben's surprise, they reached camp. When Sir Donald heard their tale, he was fascinated. "A wall of these roses, you say?" he demanded. "Packed tight together?"

"Like in the tale of Sleeping Beauty, sir," Ben said.

Sir Donald's eyes lit up. "Why, it would be the perfect defence against predators! Who knows what we might find in there? Perhaps an entire new ecosystem!"

Dinner was postponed. Sir Donald recruited ten porters with machetes and Miguel and Ben led the way to the wall of roses.

"We never catch dinner now," Miguel muttered. Under his supervision, the machete-bearers were hacking their way through the blood rose thicket. They were making such a racket that the deer would have long since fled.

Sir Donald patted him on the back. "Never mind, Miguel! Think what we might be contributing to knowledge!"

Miguel's expression showed quite clearly what he thought of the edible qualities of knowledge, but he said nothing.

The porters had hacked a tunnel as high as a man through about ten feet of blood rose. Suddenly one of their blades clanged against stone. The porter cautiously poked his machete through the remaining stems and pulled them away from the stone. Then he called out in Spanish and stepped back so that Sir Donald could see.

The biologist came forward and looked closely at the stone. He took a machete of his own and used it to push the thorns aside. Ben peered curiously over his shoulder. A snarling, stone face gazed out.

Ben gasped and Sir Donald exclaimed, "By George! Miguel! Send a man to fetch Señor Cole and Señor Sherwood, quickly!"

By the time the two other scientists arrived, the porters had uncovered about ten square feet of wall. It was covered with the organic shapes of Mayan hieroglyphics: rounded images of heads, hands, feet and unidentifiable objects. They were arranged together in clusters of twos and threes, and the clusters were organized in rows, like a grid.

Elsewhere the porters had uncovered a large, pointed, stone ear, obviously part of a much larger carving than the rest of the hieroglyphics. They kept working to reveal the top of the head and the other ear. Then two large, glaring eyes. Ben could see that the carving was the head of a large bat. The head was about five feet high, so it must have gone all the way down to the ground behind the roses.

Harrison Cole stared at the carvings in awe. "Astounding!" he said. "What is this place? A temple?"

"Perhaps. . ." Uncle Edwin ran his hands over the stone. "But this isn't a building. It's a natural lump of rock, probably limestone."

"Yet someone carved all this," Harrison said. "They must have had a reason. . ."

Ben felt a happy sense of relief spread through him as he listened to the men chatting. They had discovered something special, everyone was happy and no one blamed him for scaring off the deer. What could be better?

His father drew out his notebook and started copying down the hieroglyphic inscriptions as fast as he could. Uncle Edwin was examining the rock from every angle, trying to get a clue as to the purpose of the site. And then another cry went up from the porters who had uncovered the top half of the bat's head. They had found the bat's mouth.

And the mouth wasn't carved. It was an opening in the rock. The bat glared out of the stone at the explorers and its mouth was a dark, round hole.

Edwin crouched down and ran his fingers around the edge of the opening. "I'd say this was a natural cave," he declared. "The edges are rough. It might connect with a much larger cave system below. The whole peninsula is riddled with caverns. The Ancient Mayans must have carved the bat's head around the cave entrance. I'd say this place *must* be religious."

"Did the Mayans have a bat god?" Ben asked.

Edwin Sherwood grinned. "Why, yes. Remember my statue? Their bat god was—"

"Camazotz!" Uncle Edwin and Miguel said the word together – although Miguel seemed to spit it out in disgust.

"Camazotz!" Several of the porters repeated the word fearfully and backed away from the cave.

"What was Camazotz like?" Ben inquired.

"He was—" Harrison Cole began.

"*El Diablo!*" Miguel snapped. "An evil, evil god. The god of blood and of death – He Who Walks by Darkness. Señors, this is a bad place!"

El Diablo, Ben thought. *The Devil*. He looked at the cave with interest.

"Oh, come, Miguel," Ben's father chided. "We are rational men. We don't believe—"

"No, no one believe," Miguel interrupted angrily. "But

this land belong to the old gods. You think they go away because your missionaries say so? Oh no! They wait. They sleep. But still they survive!" He turned and stalked away.

Sir Donald was paying no attention to any of this. He was bending down and peering into the darkness. "All kinds of things are found in caves," he mused. "A nice, safe environment – doubly safe, with those roses to protect it. Who's coming with me?"

"Take Ben, Sir Donald," Harrison suggested. "My place is out here with these carvings."

"And I want to scout around the area," said Uncle Edwin. "This might be the centre of a temple complex."

Ben badly wanted to go into the cave – but he would have preferred more company. He looked at the carving again and shivered. On its own, the cave would have been an innocent hole in the rock. With the bat's head etched around the outside, it looked sinister and forbidding.

"Ben?" Sir Donald asked hopefully, and Ben silently chided himself. He was twelve years old and this was the nineteenth century. So he put on a smile.

"Of course, Sir Donald!" he replied brightly.

Sir Donald lit a lamp and crawled into the cave, which was awkward because one hand had to hold the lantern ahead of him. Ben waited for him to move on, then followed on his hands and knees. He felt cool, damp air against his face – a blessed relief from the jungle's humidity.

He could see the light of the lantern flickering ahead and crawled towards it. He was in a short, rocky passage with a rough floor. It curved and suddenly opened into a much larger cavern. Ben stood up gingerly. There was plenty of room now and the air was marvellously cool, but there was a musky animal smell that was almost overpowering. The cavern was large and low, and the lamp cast a small circle of light that didn't reach the walls. Ben couldn't see any animals.

Sir Donald was staring up at the ceiling, lantern held high. His mouth was wide open beneath his bushy moustache. "Splendid!" he murmured. "Absolutely splendid!"

Ben looked up, and was startled to see tiny red eyes looking back at him. He cried out in surprise – the ceiling was covered with bats.

The shout echoed around the cave and Sir Donald pressed his finger to his lips. "Hush, Ben," he whispered. "We don't want them to swarm."

The bats didn't seem to be disturbed, which was fortunate. Ben tried to imagine what it would be like, standing in this cave while the bats fluttered around – their black, leathery wings brushing against him.

Ben guessed that there must have been about a hundred bats. They hung upside down from the cave roof, packed so tightly together that Ben couldn't see the stone. Their wings and their fur were so dark, it was as if they sucked in the light from the lamp.

Ben had seen colonies of bats before but somehow these were different. He suddenly realized why. Their eyes were open. Bats usually sleep during the day, but these ones were watching the humans below. One of them in particular seemed to have its eyes fixed on Ben. It seemed to be the biggest in the colony and its pointed ears were aimed forward. Ben thought it looked like an upside-down cat concentrating on a mouse. He nervously took a couple of steps to one side, and the bat moved its head to follow him. Ben gulped.

"Fascinating. . ." Sir Donald mused. "No fear of the light. It has to be a new species. Their shape is very similar to *Desmodus rufus*, but larger. And darker. I wouldn't mind a look at the teeth but they would probably object."

"Wha. . ." Ben had to swallow before he could speak properly. He tried to whisper and all that came out was a dry breath. "What's *Desmodus rufus*, Sir Donald?"

Sir Donald looked down at him with a cheery smile. "Vampire bat, m'boy! Several species of 'em in this part of the world. Not to worry," he added quickly, seeing Ben's expression. "They're quite harmless. Typically, they'll take a few drops of blood from cattle or horses at night, that's all."

Ben glanced up at the bats again. The big bat seemed to stare right back at him.

"Pop back out, will you, Ben? Tell the others we have work to do. We must build a fire, flood this place with smoke to knock the bats out, then collect a few specimens."

"Right-o, Sir Donald." Ben dropped back to his knees and crawled down the passageway. He had to go carefully because his own body blocked the light from the lamp behind him, but once he was round the curve he could see daylight ahead.

Suddenly there was a tremendous groaning sound and he froze. What was it? He heard a creak as if the earth around him was waking from a long sleep. . .

Something brushed against his face and Ben pawed frantically at his head. For a horrible moment he thought a bat had got caught in his hair. Then he realized it was worse. Powdered rock was trickling down from the ceiling.

"Sir Donald!" he shouted.

Sir Donald's own cry came echoing down the tunnel at the same time. "Ben! The roof is coming down! Get out!"

Ben started to crawl quickly, then immediately stopped as guilt overcame him. He couldn't just leave Sir Donald. He looked back, then looked forward again in indecision. . .

Hands grabbed his wrists and yanked him into the daylight – just as the roof of the cave came crashing down behind him.

CHAPTER FOUR

From the journal of Benedict Cole
6th March 1850 (continued)

It was Father who pulled me out. He had heard the cave starting to collapse, and he had dived straight in to get me. He dragged me out of the way of the entrance and held me tightly. He asked what on earth I had been doing, just waiting there? He was squeezing me so hard, I could hardly speak. I told him I hadn't wanted to leave Sir Donald behind, and he sighed and gave a sort of laugh and said of course I hadn't, and he was very proud of me.

Uncle Edwin asked me what we had found in there. I mentioned the bats, and Miguel overheard. He repeated, "Bats?" very loudly. And then he shouted something at the porters, too fast for me to understand any of it apart from the word "Camazotz" – and some of them turned and fled!

Thinking back, Emily, it was just the native porters

who ran, or the ones like Miquel, with Mayan blood in them. Uncle Edwin shouted after them that they were superstitious peasants. I presume they believe the terrible legends about Camazotz.

Once the dust had settled, we tried to call to Sir Donald, but we couldn't hear him. We cleared away a small pile of rubble from the entrance, but further back there was a big rock blocking the whole passage.

Ben watched as the remaining Spanish porters cut a couple of long wooden poles from a tree. Then his father and Uncle Edwin helped them wedge the poles in around the edges of the boulder, hoping to lever it out. Ben hung about on the edges of the work, almost in agony. He was worried for Sir Donald and he badly wanted to help. But Harrison had told him to keep out of the way. Ben suspected that his father didn't want him nearby in case of another rockfall.

"*Se movió!*" The shout rang out from one of the porters – *it moved!*

The men bent to their task with renewed enthusiasm. The poles were well and truly wedged in place, and the men rocked them back and forth. Suddenly the rock shifted and rolled out of the cave mouth. The men danced aside to avoid crushed ankles. A couple of them took the boulder and rolled it further out of the way. Edwin, Ben and Harrison crouched down to peer into the cave.

Ben jumped back as a cloud of debris suddenly erupted from the cave mouth. Then something moved inside and Sir Donald Finlay staggered out into the daylight, covered in dust. He paused a moment, then straightened up. The men cheered, then fell into a self-conscious silence. They looked around, frowning.

The jungle had fallen quiet.

Ben noticed it too. The jungle was usually full of noise, even at night. There were insects, there was the wind in the leaves, there were slitherings and barks and howls that you did not want to know about. But there was *always* noise. He was so used to it that he had stopped noticing it long ago.

Now he noticed it because it was gone. The silence was like something thick and heavy, laid down over the forest. Every noise he or anyone else made seemed much too loud. But Ben felt he needed to break the unnatural stillness. "Are you all right, Sir Donald?" he inquired anxiously.

Sir Donald fixed Ben with an icy stare. "I am perfectly well," he snapped, brushing the dust from his clothes. "Do not waste my time with trivial questions." He took a step forward and looked around. His gaze fell on the inscriptions at the mouth of the cave. Something like a faint, proud smile flitted across his face, but it was gone as quickly as it had come. "More importantly, the bats are also well," he continued. "A fascinating and unique species. I need specimens. Sherwood, send the men back to the camp for the crates. Tip out all the creatures so far collected – they are unimportant. Bring the crates back here. And bring thick sackcloth with you – the bats are nocturnal and must be kept in darkness."

For a moment, no one moved. They were too surprised.

Sir Donald's voice rose irritably. "Do I have to repeat myself?" he demanded.

Edwin Sherwood turned quickly to the porters and repeated the orders. He made up for his surprise with a brusqueness of his own.

Ben was standing still, stunned by Sir Donald's abrupt dismissal.

His father came over and put an arm around him. "I expect he was more shaken by the experience than he will admit, Ben," he said softly. "Time will heal it."

Ben, his father and Uncle Edwin returned to camp with the porters, leaving Sir Donald at the cave. There was no sign of Miguel and the other Mayans about the tents. They really did seem to have fled the camp.

Following Sir Donald's orders, the captured specimens were released – even Ben's beloved violaceous trogon. The porters set off back into the jungle with the now-empty boxes. Harrison Cole settled down at one of the trestle tables and started to study his copies of the inscriptions, comparing them to notes already made in his other books. Edwin Sherwood disappeared into his tent.

Ben hung around. He was at something of a loss. No specimens to look after; nothing he could do to help his father; not much he could contribute back at the cave, either. And the jungle was still completely silent, which was unsettling. When Ben could bear the tension no longer, he jumped up and walked about the clearing, longing for something to happen and break the oppressive quiet. He thought of whistling a tune, but his breath dried up before it even reached his lips.

It was dark now and the fire cast very little glow. Ben helped his father light some lanterns, but still they could barely see the edge of the clearing. It was like being alone in a dimly lit bubble at the bottom of the sea. For the first time in months, Ben felt cold and drew his jacket around him. He wondered if he was catching a fever.

A faint sound behind him made Ben turn and shout in surprise. A dark figure stood on the edge of the clearing. It came forward into the light and Benedict flushed when he saw it was only Sir Donald.

"You are very loud today," Sir Donald said coldly. "This way! Bring them here!"

The porters followed after him. They each carried crates covered with cloth, two men to a box.

"Put them there," Sir Donald ordered, pointing at the edge of the clearing. When the boxes were set down, he stepped forward and pulled the cloth off the first one. The crate was full of bats. They hung from the top of the cage, just as they had hung from the cave roof. Sir Donald moved down the row of boxes, pulling the coverings off each. They were all full. Earlier on he had said he wanted to collect a few specimens. Now it looked as if he had collected the entire cave.

And they were clearly alive and awake. The bats couldn't fly in their boxes, but Ben could see them shifting as they jostled to and fro, and their tiny blood-red eyes glittering in the firelight as they looked around.

"Weren't you going to knock them out, Sir Donald?" he asked. He remembered that, before the rockfall, Sir Donald had talked about building a fire.

"There was no need," Sir Donald replied abruptly. "They're quite tame. Don't pester me with questions."

Clearly he was still far from his usual bluff, friendly self. Ben glanced at his father, who just shrugged. Anyone could be distracted when they were occupied with something important.

Sir Donald was fiddling with the first cage and Ben wondered what he was doing. Then the door of the crate swung open and the bats swarmed out.

The Spanish porters yelled and instinctively crouched down with their hands over their heads. Ben, who had now been told off twice in one day for shouting, deliberately did *not* scream. Like a good English gentleman he held his ground, but he was poised to flee.

The bats simply flew around the clearing a couple of times, then settled. They hung from the trees and gazed down at the humans. Sir Donald opened the next cage, and the next. When he had finished, the clearing was rimmed with black bats hanging from the branches.

"As I said," Sir Donald remarked. "Quite tame."

And so the party ate its dinner in silence, under the gaze of a hundred bats. The jungle still had not resumed its usual racket, and the presence of the bats kept the humans quiet as well. The porters barely nibbled their food. Harrison tried to start a conversation, but Sir Donald would only snap a couple of words and Ben didn't feel like talking. He fancied the clearing was like a target. The bats around it were like arrows, and he felt as if he and his companions were sitting in the bullseye.

CHAPTER FIVE

From the journal of Benedict Cole
6th March 1850 (continued)

It's not hard to work out that, with all the crates full, the expedition is over. We have nothing left to store any specimens in. Uncle Edwin pointed this out at dinner, and Sir Donald said, "Indeed. Tomorrow we will head back to the coast." Father, astonished, asked him why. And he just said, "Because I choose to."

It was the first time I'd seen them disagree. Father was expecting us to be here a couple more months. Uncle Edwin said they hadn't even begun to do the real work they'd come for. Sir Donald said there would be no argument: his mind was made up, and it was his expedition. Which is true, he pays the bills, but even so. . . I could see Father's dreams crumbling as he spoke. And Uncle Edwin! I thought he was going to hit Sir Donald, only he would never do that in front of me. Father just mumbled something like, "At least we have the carvings, eh, Ben?" and let it go. You know he never likes to keep an argument going. But I know how disappointed he is.

After that we were silent for a while. I think Father and Uncle Edwin were too angry to speak. Then suddenly Sir Donald started another conversation. He asked Uncle Edwin about his famous bat statue. Uncle Edwin answered to be civil, but he was very brusque. He said that it was solid gold and about six inches across. It was in a remarkable state of preservation and was a strangely life-like depiction of a bat – not stylized like so much Mayan art. Apparently, only one other like it has been found. It was discovered two years ago by the French archaeologist Dampierre, and it's fashioned in the same style as the bat – possibly by the same craftsman. Dampierre's piece is shaped like an eye and it's kept at the Louvre in Paris.

Sir Donald asked again and again whether Uncle Edwin's bat and Dampierre's eye were the only two pieces found in that particular style. Uncle Edwin insisted that they were and, once he seemed satisfied on that count, Sir Donald stopped talking about anything else. Uncle Edwin tried to talk about more of his work but at that point Sir Donald just cut him dead.

I'll ask Father about Camazotz later – I want to know why the Mayan porters fled. I'll tell you everything he says.

* * *

"Camazotz?" said Harrison Cole later. He and Ben were in their tent preparing for bed. "He was an even-more-than-usually unpleasant Mayan god. The god of the underworld. Well, it makes sense. The Ancient Mayans believed caves lead to the underworld, and bats live in caves. But this one. . ." Harrison crouched suddenly and flapped his coat like a pair of wings. "He was a bat god who fed on human blood – a vampire! Even worse, he could turn his followers into vampires too. Then they could take the form of a bat – or assume their human shape, just as they chose. And they, too, drank human blood and turned others into vampires like themselves."

Ben spotted the flaw immediately. "But very soon, everyone would be blood-drinkers and no one else would be left!"

Harrison shrugged. "It seems he had weaknesses. You heard Miguel call him 'He Who Walks by Darkness'. Camazotz couldn't tolerate direct sunlight and neither could his servants. Doubtless they had other weaknesses, but we don't know enough about the religion to say what they were."

"I wonder if Miguel could have told us," Ben said thoughtfully.

"Ah, yes, Miguel," Harrison sighed. "Old superstitions last a long time in this part of the world, Ben. We Europeans like to think that we can bring our civilization and our religion to new lands, and everything that was here before simply vanishes. But no. Mostly the new is just absorbed into the old. Take the Day of the Dead. The Mexicans celebrate it each year and it comes straight out of the old Aztec religions to the north, but it's mixed with a heavy dose of Catholicism now.

"Beliefs in gods like Camazotz can't be absorbed into Christianity, no matter how hard you try . . . well, you saw what happens. But they don't disappear, they just lie dormant in men's minds, until the right occasion. The carvings were about Camazotz. The cave was full of bats – as any cave in this part of the world might well be. A superstitious man like Miguel needs no further confirmation that Camazotz lived there."

Ben lay silently on his camp bed for a while, thinking about the bats. Thinking about how intelligently they looked at him. But he told himself that there was no reason bats couldn't be intelligent. It was unusual, but it was not impossible. They could be clever like, say, a dog; nothing like a man, of course.

He glanced at his father, who was hunched over his notebooks, scribbling furiously, and then he settled down to sleep.

From the journal of Benedict Cole
10th March 1850

I woke to a very subdued camp today. The bats are back in their crates, but the jungle keeps its oppressive silence, and no one much feels like breaking it with chat. Sir

Donald remains brusque, although it is now three days since the accident.

It is our third night on the trail. We are heading back to port but it is still some days away. We aren't retracing the route that brought us here, which means Uncle Edwin won't get to see his ruined city for a second time. Sir Donald is leading us in what he says is a straight line through the jungle. It certainly seems straight, but when you can hardly see the sky, it's hard to tell.

The worst news is that we have an illness. We have come this far with no more than a few upset stomachs, but this sickness is more serious. Some of the porters have fallen ill and complain of exhaustion. They look utterly drained. Whatever it is, it acts quickly. Men are fit and healthy when the sun goes down, and pale and weak by morning. Overnight the skin on their faces becomes stretched tight over their skulls, and their ribs show clear beneath their skin. It seems strange to me that the illness has struck the porters rather than the Europeans, for the porters are used to this country and climate, whereas we are newcomers.

We push on, and everything we do revolves around the bats. We mustn't make a noise for fear of disturbing them. The crates must be carried just so, in order not to jostle them. The porters may not chew tobacco in case the smell offends the bats. Sir Donald still lets the bats out every evening, and they cluster round our camp and stare at us. Then, in the mornings, they are back inside the crates and *covered up again. I suppose they must feed at some point but I have never seen them do so. And it has just occurred to me: how does Sir Donald intend to keep them alive on the sea crossing?*

"Anaemia," declared Edwin Sherwood decisively. He straightened up from the body and looked around at the porters who were gathered about him. He wasn't a doctor, but he was a wealthy Englishman and Ben knew that that alone gave him authority.

The camp had woken as usual, to find the bats back in their crates and Sir Donald impatient to move on. Some of the ill men groaned; their skin drawn ever tighter over their bones. But from one bedroll, there was not a sound or sign of movement. The man had died overnight.

"Anaemia," Harrison Cole agreed, nodding vigorously. "It can't be anything else. A very common condition and – Ben! What are you doing? Get back!"

Ben was drawn by an irresistible and horrified fascination. He had never seen a dead man before. The man's face was as white as paper and he lay peacefully – as if he had died without any kind of struggle. Ben's father had closed his eyes so that it looked as if the man was just lying there on the ground. But he wasn't. Whatever it was that had made him alive was gone.

Ben drew back, thinking about the dead man. If he had a family, his wife and children would never see him again. With just this one death, of a man whose name Ben didn't even know, something irreplaceable had vanished from the world.

"He have what we have," said one of the porters, his voice tired and weak. The obvious thought had occurred to him and probably to the others. "We will die, too?"

"No one need die," replied Edwin Sherwood brusquely. "Sir Donald has the right idea. We need to get out of this jungle, so strike the camp and we'll be off – after we've buried, um. . ."

"Juan," put in the porter, expressionlessly.

"Juan. Of course," Edwin agreed.

Sir Donald hadn't been involved in any of this. He was off to one side, looking at his bats. Harrison Cole went over and told him they were going to hold a funeral. He asked whether, as leader of the expedition, Sir Donald would like to say a word at the grave.

Ben saw Sir Donald stare blankly at his father. "Perform whatever death rituals you must, Cole," he said, "for all the good it will do." He walked away.

From the journal of Benedict Cole
3rd April 1850

There have been more deaths since the first. They all happen overnight. They all happen in exactly the same way. And they all happen to the porters.

Of course, Sir Donald insists on keeping all the bats.

When we didn't even have enough porters to carry them, he just put more bats into fewer crates.

Father asked Sir Donald why he didn't just leave some of the cages behind and Sir Donald exploded! He shouted that he was in charge of this expedition, that the bats were important and that he had to get every one of them back home. Father suggested that surely he just needed a couple of breeding pairs. Or that perhaps he could kill a couple to take back as specimens until another expedition, better equipped and with more men, could come back to Mexico and collect the rest.

You should have seen how angry Sir Donald was then! I thought he would choke. But eventually all he did was repeat that the bats were valuable. He said they might be the only ones of their kind in the world, and if we left them we might never find them again.

Finally, Father got angry too. He didn't shout like Sir Donald, but he asked if the bats are more important than human lives. Sir Donald replied that they are worth every sacrifice this expedition can make – down to its last man!

After that, as Uncle Edwin pointed out to Father when he thought I wasn't listening, there was just no point in trying to reason with Sir Donald any more. They are wondering if Sir Donald has a fever himself. Uncle Edwin says fevers can turn the brain.

Father and Uncle Edwin have finally learnt that I hear a lot more than they realized. Now they take great care to hold private conversations well away from me. I know it's because they don't want me to worry.

But, Emily, I can do plenty of worrying on my own. I can tell they don't believe that this illness is anaemia. The other day I heard them muttering that there are eight pints of blood in the human body, and yet the dead men have hardly any left in their veins. The remaining porters (all of whom are now ill) don't believe it either. I'm sure they only stay with us because they would feel even less safe in the jungle on their own.

I wonder what explanation Father will come up with for the latest little oddity to hit our expedition.

You see, since we entered the jungle, I've been writing these entries at night, after the day's duties are done and before I go to bed. I'm now writing this just before sunrise. Why should that be?

Because, Emily, yesterday our porters found a new way to fall ill. We are close to the edge of the jungle now. The trees are thinning out and sunbeams occasionally shine through. I've never seen a more welcome sight. But the first native who walked into the light screamed and fell back. In about two seconds he'd got the worst case of sunburn I've ever seen. His skin was bright red and blistering. I could swear it was smoking.

Sir Donald immediately called a halt. He said that from now on, we would march by night and sleep by day. The cool air is better for his bats apparently. In fact, he even insisted that we retreat a bit further back into the jungle where the trees are thicker before we set up camp.

Father and Uncle Edwin wanted to argue the point, but Sir Donald wasn't listening. He was too busy covering the crates up with cloth, making sure that no sunlight could get in.

But we can't avoid the sun for ever. We are near the sea! There is no high ground here, so we can't see it, but I can smell it. There was a good easterly breeze this afternoon and the sweet sea air smelt pure and clean. Sir Donald announced that the expedition would reach Puerto Morelos within twenty-four hours – one more night march and we are there. Sir Donald's precious bats can be stored in the deepest part of the ship's hold, well away from the sunlight (I frankly hope someone throws the wretched things overboard) and we can resume a daylight existence as God intended.

I can see daylight through the canvas. I will try to sleep now.

Ben closed his journal and stretched. He tucked it into his coat pocket and stood up.

Then he threw himself to the ground as a shot rang out. It sounded frighteningly close – just outside the tent.

Through the canvas came a hubbub of shouts, cries and screams, then a whole barrage of shots. Wide-eyed, Ben crawled to the tent flap but at that moment it was pulled open and his father stumbled in. He tripped over Ben and fell to the ground.

"Get up, Ben! Come on!" Harrison urged as he

scrambled to his feet and pulled Ben up by his collar. "We must leave. Now." He was perspiring, breathing heavily, and his face was white from fright or shock. Red blood stained his shirt collar.

"But. . ." said Ben.

"*Now*," Harrison Cole commanded. "Come on!" And he dragged Ben out at the back of the tent.

The screams were still loud outside, though Ben couldn't see where they came from. They were terrible, heart-rending, full of the knowledge of death. The shots had stopped.

The tents were pitched beneath some trees, to take advantage of the shade during the day. This early, the sun was just high enough for the trees to throw shadows. All the bats were out of their cages. Some were swarming around the site, staying within the shade. Others clustered together on the ground. They looked like writhing piles of black leaves. Then, horrified, Ben saw arms and legs protruding from the piles, and he realized where the screams were coming from. The bats were feeding on the porters. All of them!

Sir Donald stood nearby, and smiled. He turned when he saw Ben and his father, and smiled even more widely. Impossibly widely. His grin seemed to split his face from ear to ear. "*Join the feast*," he said. It was not his usual voice. It was deep and harsh and guttural. It seemed to come from the air all around him.

Harrison pulled Ben out of the shade and into the

sunlight. Ben blinked as the dawn sunbeams hit his eyes.

"Run, Ben," Harrison Cole said. "The bats can't come into the light. Run!"

CHAPTER SIX

From the journal of Benedict Cole
3rd April 1850 (continued)

Father would not say a word until we had run, then
walked, then run again for an hour. We were heading
down a dusty track towards the coast. The sea breeze was
no compensation for the heat of the sun now, and we
hadn't even taken hats from the tent.

I was full of questions, Emily – bursting with them, as
I'm sure you are too. At least you can skip ahead.

By the end of the hour, Father was staggering and I
had to hold him up. We finally stopped beneath some
trees, but first Father made me climb up one of them and
look back the way we had come. Was anyone following
us? I couldn't see anyone – or anything – and I said so.
Then I jumped back down, and for the first time since
fleeing the tent I got a proper look at Father.

Oh, Emily, I can hardly bear to write it. I had thought

he was white from shock. Now I saw I had been wrong. Father was pale, but it wasn't shock. It was a symptom I had seen all too often over the last fortnight. Father had the illness.

He lay slumped against the base of the tree, and could only manage a weak smile. He told me to sit next to him, and he put an arm around me. He said, "I should never have brought you here, Ben." And then I thought he had died, because his voice trailed off and his head lolled. But he suddenly seemed to take strength and brought his head back up.

"He stopped pretending," Harrison said. His voice was very faint. Fighting back the tears in his eyes, Ben pressed close in order to catch every word. His father sighed. "It was our last camp. We would soon be at the port. He had no need to pretend any further. He had no more use for the porters, no more use for any of us, so he gave us to the bats. No more grazing, as they had been doing until now. They were to be fully fed."

Ben frowned, trying desperately to make sense of this. "Do you mean Sir Donald?" he asked.

Harrison Cole shook his head wearily. "Sir Donald is dead, Ben. He died in the cave. I mean Camazotz!"

Ben stared as his father explained.

"The legends are true. I translated the inscriptions, Ben. It was a rough interpretation, sketchy, but I could see what they meant. Of course, Edwin and I still didn't believe it! Not at first. We are modern, rational men. But bit by bit, it made sense. We saw things. There were clues – and eventually we realized. . .

"Listen, Ben, I don't know how Camazotz ended up in that cave. I don't know what he's been doing all these centuries. But I do know he possessed Sir Donald. And those bats, those infernal creatures, are his servants.

"We realized, Edwin and I, what was in store for us all. So, we confronted Camazotz in Sir Donald's form. We were fools! We thought a nineteenth-century firearm could take on a Mayan god. Edwin shot him in the chest, point blank. There was no blood. He just laughed, and the hole healed. And then the bats fell on us – Edwin and the porters and me.

"I went down under the sheer weight of them. And I felt fangs sinking into my neck. . ." He shuddered and pulled down his collar so that Ben could see the two small wounds, side by side.

"Edwin wrenched them off me and told me to get you and run. So I did. The last I saw of him, he was holding them away, shooting with his revolvers, trying to give us time to escape. He died like a hero, Ben.

"Now, listen." Harrison sounded weaker, but his tone was more urgent. "This is very important. I don't know what Camazotz is after, but if he simply wanted to wreak havoc in Mexico, he wouldn't be going to all this trouble. It's my guess he wants to get himself and his bats to London. So, here is what you must do. You must go to Puerto Morelos and catch a boat ahead of him. Tonight, sleep in a private home. Camazotz can't enter, you see, and neither can his vampires. He and his kind need an invitation to come in. That's why we were safe in our tents. They were our homes in the jungle. Then tomorrow you must get on a boat and get away—"

"Just me?" Ben burst out. "No! No, Father, you're coming too!"

"Me?" Harrison Cole's smile was very weak and tired. "Yes, of course. I'm coming too. *We* must get to Puerto Morelos. And we must get there by sunset today, or the bats will come for us. Remember, shelter in a private home. . ." He sighed, and Ben had to strain to hear him. "Very tired. Need to sleep a little. . ."

Harrison's arm tightened around Ben, and Ben hugged him back. He looked up at the sun through the trees. It was still nowhere near noon. There was plenty of time for a brief rest before they headed off for Puerto Morelos. He thought he would see if he could find some water before they set off, as the day would only get warmer.

Harrison's arm loosened about Ben's shoulders and his head lolled again so that his chin rested on his chest. Ben slipped gently away, careful not to wake him. He wondered how much blood his father had lost. . .

Harrison slowly keeled over on to the ground.

"Father?" Ben asked anxiously. He knelt down and touched him gently on the shoulder. "Father?" Before he realized it, he was shaking Harrison with both hands. Tears streamed down his face as the terrible truth sank in – his father was never going to wake up. Harrison Cole was dead.

Ben lay on the ground with his face buried in his father's shirt, and cried for a long, long time. For some reason, he particularly remembered one day when he had been playing back home, in the small park in the middle of Bedford Square. He must have been five or six years old and he had decided to climb a tree. He climbed higher and higher but then something had given way beneath his foot and he had found himself plummeting head first towards the earth. His father's strong arms had caught him, inches from the ground.

Harrison Cole had calmly set Ben upright and taken him home for lunch. After lunch he had taught his son to climb trees properly. Ben had never fallen out of a tree since.

And now there was no one to catch him, ever again.

Eventually Ben could cry no more. He thought of his father's instructions. Slowly he rose to his feet and arranged his father's body so that Harrison Cole lay peacefully on his back. Then he took Harrison's coat and laid it over his face. He knelt by the body. All he could remember of the funeral service was the Lord's Prayer, so he recited it carefully. Then he stood up.

"Goodbye, Father," Ben said in a choked voice. He

turned, and walked off down the track, heading for the coast and for home.

There are no more tears as I write this, Emily. Does that sound callous? I think Father would approve. I've done my mourning for him. Now I have my mission, and the important thing is to stay alive...

Ben entered Puerto Morelos in the middle of the afternoon, starving and parched. He had walked all the way through the heat of the midday sun. There had been streams along the way, but he had nothing to carry water in. He had taken off his jacket and wrapped it around his head, like a turban. Now he was back among people, he put it on again properly.

The small town was just as sleepy and unhurried as he remembered. The hotel was still there in the zocolo and his eyes lit up. People paid to stay there, but surely the proprietor lived there too? That made it a home, and hence impervious to Camazotz and his kind.

But Ben didn't make it to the hotel. One side of the zocolo led straight out to the fishing dock. And as he looked out towards the sea, Ben almost cheered. There was a ship there!

It wasn't the ship Sir Donald had chartered for the

voyage. The expedition wasn't expected back for another month. But this ship was British – the Union Jack flew from its stern. And another flag was flying there too. It was blue, with a white square in the centre – it was the Blue Peter, which meant that the ship was preparing to depart.

Ben forced his aching legs into a run. His feet pounded on the dry earth, then the wooden planks of the dock. The ship was a three-masted merchantman, moored on its starboard side with its stern to the town. The lettering below the cabin window said it was out of Liverpool. Sailors were still loading supplies from the dock. Clearly departure wasn't that imminent and Ben could afford to walk again.

A grizzled man was leaning on the rail of the quarterdeck, watching the activity. Ben knew from experience that only one man on a ship could afford to look inactive when all around him were busy. He walked down the dock until he was standing opposite the man. "Ahoy, captain!" he called.

The man looked round and grinned. "Well, hello, young sir," he said. "Weren't expecting an English voice here."

"Are you sailing to England?" Ben asked eagerly.

"Aye, via New York and Halifax. We sail in an hour, when the tide turns."

"Have you. . ." Ben tried to sound casual, but it came out very eagerly. "Have you room for another passenger?"

The captain suddenly looked shrewd. "Well, as you can see, we're pretty packed out. We're carrying printed Mexican textiles for the London ladies. Mebbe we could squeeze in a small chap like you. I can tell by your voice that you's a gentleman, so –" the captain leaned on the rail and narrowed his eyes – "there'd be no question about paying the fare, would there, now?"

Ben's heart sank. He was penniless!

The captain read his expression and shook his head. "Thought as much. I can't hand out free tickets, young sir. Bad for business," he said.

"I-I. . ." Ben stammered. "I could work my way. Earn my passage. Be a cabin boy."

The captain grinned. "To look at you, I'm guessing you ain't worked your way too often before, right?"

Ben's face burned. "But I—" he began.

The captain shook his head again. "Sorry, son. If you's running away from your dad, you won't do it on my boat." He spat into the water and turned away from the rail.

Ben stepped back from the ship, his face flushing with embarrassment. He felt like the world's biggest fool. And worse than that was the way it brought home his new station in life. He was a penniless orphan in a foreign country. No one owed him anything. And Ben felt powerless.

But then Ben remembered his father's words and a new determination flared within him – he wasn't completely powerless after all, and there were more ways to get onboard a ship than to go up the gangplank.

CHAPTER SEVEN

From the journal of Benedict Cole
3rd April 1850 (continued)

So, this is how I became a criminal, Emily. I had no choice but to stow away.

I was surprised at myself. Even as I turned away from the ship, I knew exactly what I was going to do. I could see it all lying ahead of me, as clearly as the track that had brought me into town.

The first step was to study the ship. The captain had already forgotten about me. I strolled casually along the dock to study the decks. There was no raised forecastle or poop, like an old-fashioned man-of-war. The deck was smooth from stem to stern. There were three square-rigged masts and two things like huts, which I thought covered the stairways down below – that would be where the cabins were. There was a large hatch in the middle of the deck that I thought led directly to the hold.

What interested me most was the foredeck, the area right at the front of the ship. The ship's boat was stowed there. Because of that, and the forward stairwell cover that I mentioned, no one further astern could see what went on there. That suited me.

The second step was to get provisions. I took off my coat and hid it at the end of the dock. Father would have been shocked at my appearance, but in a white, open-necked shirt (that needs a good clean) at least I looked a little more like a local. And then I crept around the back of the stalls in the market and stole food.

I took nothing that would perish quickly. Mostly biscuit — and limes, because I've heard about scurvy. I think it will be enough for about two weeks, if I eat sparingly. The captain said he was stopping at New York. Once there, I can either steal some more, or turn myself in to the British consul. He will _have_ to send me home. I also stole a pair of water flasks and unblushingly filled them up at a water-trough (well out of sight of their original owner), as though nothing could be more natural.

The third step was to head casually back to the dock. I retrieved my coat and wrapped the food up in it. There was a pile of fishing baskets that hid me from the ship. I sat down behind it and dangled my feet over the edge of the dock. I tied my coat around my neck by the sleeves, so that the bundle dangled against my shoulders. Then I leaned forward quickly and heaved myself over the side.

I slid down into the sea with a splash. Fortunately my

coat stayed dry or the food – and this journal – would have been ruined. I quickly paddled under the dock, using only breaststroke so that my arms and legs wouldn't splash. Now I wished I had taken off my boots, for they were heavy and dragged my feet down.

The ship was on my left. I swam slowly down the dock, underneath the planking, past the ship and up to the bow. Then I made my way round to the port side, which was facing out to sea. The anchor was directly above me. It was lashed to the side of the ship and its cable disappeared into a hole in the side. The anchor was too far up for me to reach from the water, but I climbed up a chain, got a foot up on to the anchor and swung myself over. My heart was in my mouth, because one slip would have sent me back into the drink with a loud splash that was bound to be noticed.

But no. I dangled from the anchor and got my feet up over the tines. I had to push my bundle through the cable hole first, then wriggle in after it. There was just room for me to push my way through.

And here I am in my new home – the cable locker. Neither of the anchors is in use, so there is no reason why anyone should come in here for the duration of the voyage. It's smaller than I thought it would be, and it's full of stacks of coiled rope, standing on slatted racks to dry. It's too low even for me to stand. Part of the ceiling is a grating in the deck, but the rest is solid, so there is shade and I can hide away from prying eyes.

I can't stay in here for ever, of course, but it's April and I won't freeze to death. Eventually my supplies will run out. When they do, I'll creep out at night and find more. Then, when we are halfway across the Atlantic, closer to home than to anywhere else, I will emerge and reveal myself. They will have to take me to England then.

It is far from perfect, but it is also infinitely better than the alternative. The captain said the ship would be sailing in an hour. Most of that hour must be up by now. Goodbye, Mexico – for ever, I hope.

Later

I can't believe it! The wind has changed!

I actually heard it. It picked up across the water – an eerie, whooshing noise. I peered out through the cable hole and saw the wave tops being ruffled by the wind. And then it hit the ship. I felt the force: it was a very gentle blow, but the ship creaked as if protesting, and bumped into the dock.

And here we are, still. It must be hours later because the sun has just gone down. All I can tell is what I overhear from any crew that are nearby. One was saying he'd never known anything like this – a squall so steady as to hold a ship in place for hours. There are no tugs in Puerto Morelos. The crew could get into the ship's boat and tow, but apparently no one thinks that would work against a wind this strong. So, we are being held against the dock, and we won't be able to leave until the wind changes direction again—

"Ahoy, ship!"

The cry was very faint, but Ben froze in mid-sentence. *It couldn't be!* he thought, and scrambled across to the starboard side to press his face against the cable hole. As he struggled to see what was happening, he barely noticed that the wind had suddenly died away and the ship was no longer being held at the dock. The hole faced forward and he couldn't see anything further astern, but he could hear the voices without any possibility of mistake.

It no longer mattered that the wind had changed – Sir Donald had caught up with the ship.

From the journal of Benedict Cole
4th April 1850

Again, I can only repeat what I overheard from the sailors.

Sir Donald (well, Camazotz in Sir Donald's body) turned up on the dockside with a cart packed full with covered crates. I heard him call "Permission to come on board, sir?" myself. I don't know quite what the captain said, but it wasn't enough, because Sir Donald said it again, and then again. Eventually I heard the captain shout, "Confound it, sir, yes, you have permission to come on board!"

Sailors live on this ship. It's their home. I suppose that means that even here, Camazotz needs an invitation to enter.

I wondered what he would make of New York and Halifax, but it turns out they are no longer on the schedule. He has promised the captain five thousand pounds if the ship heads straight for London. It's twice what he expected to make from the voyage, so of course the captain has agreed.

We are at sea, at last. We just caught the end of the tide. I am trapped on a ship with Camazotz and a hundred vampires!

I can hear the sea rushing by below me, only a few feet away. When the ship leans over, spray comes rushing up the cable hole nearest the sea and I have to move over to the other side. I long to creep out and hide away in the hold, but when the feeding starts – as I have no doubt it will – I would be found. My only hope is to stay here, where no one will think of looking. By keeping quiet I am probably surrendering the entire crew to the predations of Sir Donald, but what else can I do, Emily?

5th April 1850

It is nearing the end of our first full day at sea. A strong stern wind conveniently blows us in whatever direction we need to be heading. The sailors are delighted – they have never known anything like it – although I'm sure the wind that held us to the dock came from exactly the same source.

Sir Donald is controlling the weather.

I only have the ship's bells with which to mark the time. I eat when the men eat, so I know my meals are regular. I take just a little nibble, just enough to stop my stomach growling, because I must make the food last. Eventually I will have to go out into the ship, but I want to do that as little as possible.

My two flasks of water won't last me all the way to London. But in the mornings the ship is heavy with dew – fresh water, not salt. Some of it trickles down into the locker and I put the flasks out to catch the few drops that come my way. Then I take only the smallest sips at mealtimes. The thirst is killing me, but I think it would be better to die that way...

13th April 1850

We are through the Florida Straits and past the Bahamas, which means we're well into the Atlantic Ocean. My heart is heavy. I remember the chart from our outward journey. Getting from Puerto Morelos out into the Atlantic was the only part that involved much manoeuvring. There were islands, tides and reefs to watch out for. For that, a ship needs a healthy crew. Now we have three thousand miles of open sea ahead of us. I am afraid that the ship can spare a man or two...

* * *

17th April 1850

It's started. Today I heard one of the sailors mention a strange illness. The captain has doubled the fruit ration. He must know it's not scurvy, but I remember Father and Uncle Edwin calling it anaemia. A man in authority must pretend he knows what is going on. What the captain would do if he knew the truth about the vampire plague on board his ship, heaven only knows.

19th April 1850

I think Sir Donald is following the same pattern as before. He keeps to the night and the darkness. I never see him venture on deck during daylight. His vampires are only feeding on a few hardy individuals. If everyone came down with this "illness" then the captain might head for port. But it's only one or two sailors, so the healthy ones can convince themselves that they won't get it.

And the ship sails on.

25th April 1850

The first death came last night and the captain conducted the burial at sea, early this morning before the sun was up. I had to stuff my sleeve in my mouth to stop myself crying out when "Sir Donald" was asked to say a few words.

He gave a very moving speech. He is not a fool. In the jungle, he could be as cold and aloof as he wanted. He only needed us to carry his crates. Here at sea, he needs the sailors. He is polite and friendly towards them. For now.

28th April 1850

Today I heard the point of no return announced. We are halfway across the Atlantic, closer to home than to anywhere else. Even if the ship were now consumed by the Black Death, the captain would still head for England. It's nearest.

This was the point where I had planned to come out of hiding. Now, I think not.

30th April 1850

My food is all gone. I haven't eaten for forty-eight hours. I _must_ go out and see what I can find, but I'm leaving my journal in a coil of rope. If they take me and I don't return, I pray it falls into the hands of someone who can take the right action. Please deliver this to Miss Emily Cole, Bedford Square, Bloomsbury, London.

Ben tucked the nub of pencil away in his pocket. Moonlight shone down through the grating above him and speckled the dark shapes of the coiled ropes. He had come to regard them as his friends. They shared his silent vigil.

He swallowed, braced himself and reached up. His fingers closed around the grating.

Ben would have preferred to go out by day, when the vampires were dormant. But sadly there was no direct way out of the cable locker into the rest of the ship, so he would have to climb out and cross the deck to the stairs. During the day this would have been impossible to do without being spotted by the sailors. At night there was less activity and Ben knew it would be easier for him to slip across the deck unnoticed.

He pushed, then grunted and pushed harder. The grating was well wedged into place, but it shifted and then popped out. Ben immediately froze so that it rose no more than an inch above the deck. Cautiously, he pushed it to one side and poked his head out.

For a moment he felt almost euphoric. His world had been so cramped for so long that even the brief length of the ship seemed to represent unbridled freedom. The dark night stretched away into infinity. He was at the very front of the vessel, and as he remembered, the upturned ship's boat was lashed to the deck just in front of him. It gave him cover as he crawled out on to the deck.

Ben could see figures moving about towards the stern: the helmsman at the wheel and the rest of the on-watch crew. He glanced up. There might be a lookout in the crow's nest, but no one else on deck this far forward.

Looking back down again, his eyes lit on a metal chimney that stuck out of the deck. It was an iron tube, just a bit too wide for him to get his hands around, and it was covered with a cap to keep the spray out. Ben guessed it would be the chimney for the ship's stove, which meant the galley was underneath.

Ben slid along the runnels to the forward stairwell. He had used to love this: a ship in the dark, the waves rushing by, the vessel plunging ahead into the night. There was no feeling like it. Now, all he knew was that there were predators on board whose ability to see in the dark was considerably better than his own.

He peered cautiously down the stairwell. It led into a dim wooden passage, lit by just one lantern. There was no one there. The passage was lined with slatted doors, and the stern end was shrouded in gloom.

One soft step at a time, Ben crept down the open stairs. The passage had that strange, otherworldly quality of a sailing vessel's below-decks. It looked solid, but it moved with the rest of the ship. It was slanted to starboard as the boat leaned against the wind. The hull creaked and moved around him as it pitched through the waves. The galley would be about twenty feet down on his left, which made it the second entrance. . .

The door was open! Ben inched forward and froze when he heard a sound.

He couldn't immediately place it. It wasn't the sound

of a cook at work – no chopping, stirring or clanking of pots. It wasn't conversation either. He slid down the wooden wall and peered in.

Ben bit his tongue to stop himself gasping, or crying out.

A sailor in a dirty apron sat sprawled in a chair, his head lolling back. A man crouched over him, his mouth to the sailor's neck. The man was dressed in strange robes that Ben guessed were Mayan.

He remembered what his father had said: . . .*they could take the form of a bat – or assume their human shape.*

Ben slid quickly away down the corridor and hid in the shadows at the forward end of the passage. Five minutes later, a bat flew out of the galley and down towards the stern. Ben gave it a good long while to get out of sight, then hurried quickly back to the galley.

He tried to ignore the cook's dead eyes as he packed his pockets full of food and filled his flasks with fresh water. When he had finished he took one last look at the dead man, then turned away sadly and hastened back to his hiding place.

From the journal of Benedict Cole
23rd May 1850

We've sighted Land's End, for what it's worth. How many of the crew are still alive, I don't know. The funerals stopped long ago. The bodies are just thrown overboard now, by those who are left.

I can see England, but it's still too far to swim. I would freeze or drown. The sailors know this. It's the only reason they stay on board.

The wind is blowing too strongly for us to change course. There are not enough men to manage the sail so we're heading straight up the Channel. I have a strange feeling the wind will change just enough to blow us through the Dover Strait, round Broadstairs and up the Thames Estuary.

My food is all gone again. I haven't left the locker since that first expedition and I don't dare now. London is so close.

I'm coming home, Emily.

CHAPTER EIGHT

Far away, a clock struck midnight. Ben blinked at Jack and remembered he was back in London. Ben's story had taken a long time to tell but neither boy had noticed.

Jack simply sat and stared at his new friend. It was a clear night and the courtyard was bathed in pale moonlight. Ben was strangely lit in glowing shades of white and grey. The moon had moved across the sky and even the docks were quietening down for the night. Jack had never heard a stranger tale.

"And here I am," said Ben.

"At least you made it," Jack remarked.

"Yes, *I* made it!" Ben replied. "But I'm the only one who did. Sir Donald couldn't work the sails on his own. So he left just enough sailors alive to bring down the sails and get the ship into the Thames Estuary." He choked. "I heard the screams of the last ones to go. The poor souls must have thought they had made it. Land was so close."

"But the bats got them?" asked Jack. He remembered the horror, whatever it was, that had frightened the harbour master off the ship.

"The bats got them," Ben agreed. "And now Camazotz is here."

"Yup," Jack said. "Now he's here." He looked up and around him with a renewed respect. He had grown up in London. He thought he knew it all. But it was suddenly so much more interesting. "Well, then, tell me where this 'Sir Donald' lives, and we'll go and stop him. That's your mission, ain't it?"

"Yes." Ben looked at Jack doubtfully. "It would have been a lot easier if Father had told me how."

"So what do you want to do?" Jack queried.

"Go home," Ben said and stood up slowly. "I'm going to go home, see Emily, get a decent meal – with no offence to your good friend, Molly – have a bath and sleep for about a century in a warm, comfortable bed. And if London's still standing when I'm done, then I'll worry about Sir Donald."

"*We'll* worry," Jack corrected him. He loved London and had no intention of seeing it taken over by a blood-sucking Mayan god. "It's our problem."

Ben smiled a weak but grateful smile. "Thank you," he said. "Now, can you direct me to Bedford Square?"

"Hmm." Jack put his chin in his hand and looked thoughtfully at the other boy. "So how was you thinking of managing this happy reunion? Walk up to the front door and ring the bell?"

"What else?" asked Ben, surprised.

Jack smothered a laugh and led Ben over to a darkened window. There was enough light from the moon for both boys to see their reflections clearly.

Ben gasped when he saw the ragged picture he presented. "I look like a beggar!" he exclaimed.

"You ain't Bloomsbury's finest," Jack agreed. "Go ringing bells and you'll get arrested, that's what. And your housekeeper's going to want to know where your dad is."

Ben glared at him, then turned back to study his reflection. "I have crossed thousands of miles of ocean in the company of a bloodthirsty demon," he said. "I will not be stopped by a little grime. I will find a way to speak to Emily, and not let Mrs Mills know what has happened. Come on!" And with that, he started walking.

Jack stayed where he was.

Ben stopped and looked round. "Well?" he said. "Are you coming?"

"'Course I am," Jack replied. "Only, it's this way. . ."

Jack was surprised by his friend's renewed energy. He led Ben along the river to the new London Bridge, where they crossed the Thames into the City.

London's moon-washed cobbled streets were already coming alive again. The ladies and gentlemen who had

London's money in their pockets might sleep till dawn, but the armies of tradesmen and servants who made their comfortable lives possible were already stirring. There was nothing at all unusual about two boys walking along a street in the early hours.

Ben looked around him with amazement. He had never seen this side of London's existence. At first he stayed in the shadows, for fear of whoever or whatever might see him, but soon there was such a crowd about – men and women coming and going – that he felt able to walk in the open with confidence.

They walked up Cheapside and past St Paul's. The cathedral towered over them, ghostly and beautiful in the moonlight.

Ben paused and looked up at it.

"You all right?" Jack asked.

"I was just thinking of the temples I've seen," Ben replied, "where humans were once sacrificed. I promise never to complain about long, boring church services again."

A horse-drawn milk cart clattered up the cobbles behind them. Jack showed Ben how to hitch a lift. The boys ran behind it, caught hold of the rear end and swung themselves up. The cart got them as far as Holborn before it headed on to the west and they had to jump off. From there it was only a short walk to the heart of Bloomsbury.

They reached Bedford Square as the sun was coming

up. It was not the kind of place where Jack would normally linger. The square was surrounded by tall, elegant buildings. In the middle was a green park, lined with trees and enclosed by ornate iron railings. It was still too early for the locals to be up and about, but Jack could picture it as it would be once the tradesmen had made their deliveries and withdrawn for the day. Beautiful women would promenade in their fancy bonnets and long dresses that swept the ground. Smart men in tall hats and frock coats would escort them. Here, all was peace and tranquillity, a world removed from his own existence.

"There it is," said Ben. They stood in the shadow of one of the trees. The Coles' house was a tall, thin, three-floored building on the north side of the square. It had white windows and a green door. The bricks were dark with soot, like everywhere in London. His voice shook suddenly. "It's so close."

Jack looked at the house. "So what do we do now?"

"We wait," Ben told him, and he drew back into the bushes.

They must have waited for a good two hours. Jack heard the clocks striking eight o'clock. Eventually the front door opened and two people emerged. One was a portly, middle-aged woman, dressed in black. Her skirt was not quite as fancy as the ones Jack had imagined, but it still swept the ground. She had a bonnet drawn tight around her face. The other, Jack guessed, was Emily. She was a girl about the same height as Ben, and Jack remembered being told she was a year older. She wore a pretty dress of blue and white, and had long, auburn hair. "Who's the old one?" Jack whispered.

"That's Mrs Mills," Ben answered.

"She looks like she wanted to suck a lemon, only it sucked her instead," Jack commented.

Ben smiled. "She's a good sort. She's looked after both of us since we were born."

"Where are they going?" asked Jack.

"This will be their morning walk," Ben replied. "If they're doing what they usually do, they'll just walk around the square."

Sure enough, that was what the two ladies seemed to be doing. The boys watched from the bushes. It seemed a pointless activity to Jack. Why walk unless you were going somewhere?

"I want you do to me a favour, Jack," Ben said after a while.

"What?"

"Grab Mrs Mills's bag and make a run for it."

"*What?*"

Ben gave an innocent shrug. "She will run after you and I can talk to Emily."

"And every copper in the West End will be running after me, too! You talks to Emily, I goes to Newgate Prison. No fear."

Ben looked despairing. "But I have to talk to her!"

"And you will, you will." Jack gave him a friendly pat. "But you been hanging around blood-suckers so long, it's addling your mind. Your place got a back door?"

In fact, the back door was at the front. A flight of stone steps led down to the servants' entrance. The boys quickly hurried down, out of view of the street.

Jack looked thoughtfully at the black wooden door, and at the window next to it. He would smash the glass, reach inside and open the catch. He stooped down, picked up a stone and drew back his arm.

"Hey!" Ben caught him just in time. "Now who's addled? Do you think Mrs Mills is the only staff here?" He put his finger to his lips, then leaned against the door and pressed his ear to the wood. "Tillet, Evans and Cook. I think they're all in the kitchen. Probably having a cup of tea."

"You *think*?" Jack said.

But Ben was already turning the handle, slowly and carefully. He pushed and the door opened.

"It ain't locked!" Jack whispered.

"Not when there's someone in the house, no," said Ben. "Come on."

The door led into a narrow, low corridor. Pipes ran overhead and the floor was paved with stone. There was another door on the right and Jack could hear voices behind it.

Jack and Ben tiptoed past the door and on to a flight

of stairs. The steps were narrow and wooden, with a threadbare carpet. They hurried up quickly, and at the top Ben opened a door into another world.

It was the hallway of the Coles' house, the floor on to which the front door opened. There was a plush red carpet and elaborate gold flock wallpaper. A chandelier hung from the ceiling and the walls were lined with portraits. A grandfather clock ticked sleepily in the background and tall potted plants, as big as Ben, lined the space between the servants' door and the stairs. The front door was surrounded by stained glass, and the sun shining through it lit the hallway in glorious shades of blue and green and orange.

Jack stood and gaped in frank amazement. He thought there was probably more wealth in this hallway than he would ever see in his life, and this wasn't even a room that did anything. It was just somewhere people passed through to go somewhere else.

Ben was already at the stairs. "This way!" he hissed.

Jack followed him, then paused when he saw the portrait at the stairs' foot. It showed a man and a woman, a little boy who was obviously a younger Ben, and a young girl. Ben had the same fair hair and grey eyes as his father. The girl had the same eyes too, but her auburn hair came from her mother. The man had an arm around each child, and the kindest face Jack had ever seen. It touched something inside him and he couldn't look away.

Shadows loomed suddenly on the other side of the front door. He heard the rattle of the catch and pelted after Ben. He took the stairs two at a time and the boys reached the first floor just as they heard the front door opening below.

The landing was very like the hallway, though the carpet was cream and gold. Jack felt as if he was soiling it just by being there. Ben beckoned him into a room.

"Go and take your coat off, Miss Emily," said a woman's voice below them. Despite Jack's first impression of Mrs Mills, she sounded friendly – friendly, but stern. "Then it will be time for your studies," the woman continued.

"Yes, Mrs Mills," a girl's voice replied.

Jack and Ben waited behind the door as they heard footsteps on the stairs. Jack looked around and knew this must be Emily's bedroom. Gossamer curtains hung by the window. There was a bed in one corner, surrounded by four posts and covered with a frilly counterpane. Dressers lined the walls and a large wardrobe stood directly opposite them.

Jack suddenly stiffened with surprise when he thought he saw two other boys lurking on the other side of the room. Then he realized it was only his own reflection, and Ben's, in a large mirror set in the wardrobe door.

The footsteps drew closer and the door opened. Emily walked into the room, unbuttoning her coat. She stopped suddenly when she, too, saw the reflections. She opened her mouth to scream.

Jack had already shoved the door closed. Now he leaped forward, grabbed Emily and put his hand over her mouth. She did scream, but it was muffled by his palm and no one outside the room would have heard it. She wriggled and writhed, and then slammed her heel hard into his foot. He yelped, but clenched his teeth and held on.

"Em! *Em!* It's me!" Ben had jumped in front of them. He was whispering as loudly as he dared. "It's me! It's Ben!"

Emily stopped wriggling and stared at him, her eyes enormous above Jack's hand.

Jack cautiously released her, ready to pounce on her again if she looked like making a noise. He need not have worried.

"Ben? Ben!" Emily fell into Ben's arms and they hugged each other tightly. "But you're supposed to be in Mexico! And you smell!" She turned round suddenly and glared at Jack. "And who are you?"

"The best friend your brother's got," Jack said simply.

"We'll explain, Em, I promise," Ben told her. He glanced at Jack, and Jack discreetly withdrew to a far corner of the room. Ben put an arm round his sister and led her away to the window.

Jack watched them, surprised to feel a pang of jealousy at their closeness. He knew what Ben was going to tell her and he didn't envy his friend. He remembered the portrait – the family group dominated by their father, Harrison Cole. Emily needed to know that the heart of that family had just been torn out.

This was the first time Jack had been close to a family. Emily and Ben were two people with separate minds, but so much in common. Their upbringing, their childhood together, meant they could share things in a way he never had, with anyone. He had always prized his independence. For the first time in his life, he wondered if he hadn't got the worst end of the deal.

Ben bent his head and spoke quietly. After a moment, Emily gasped. Then she flung her arms round Ben and began to sob. Ben comforted her and did not sob, though his eyes streamed.

Jack bit his lip and looked away.

CHAPTER NINE

Jack reflected on the strange change in his fortunes over the last week as he handed over a pound note to the bookseller. He very rarely saw a pound note at all, and it was more usual for other people to be giving money to him, without their realizing. But five nights ago he had met Ben Cole, and now it looked like his old life was gone.

At first he had tried to leave, but Ben and Emily had both asked him to stay – so he did. Privately, he hadn't seen what on earth he could contribute and he didn't expect it to last. But he was needed almost immediately. He could be a third mind, a voice of practical reason as they discussed plans for dealing with Sir Donald. And Ben was weak, still recovering from his ordeal. Someone healthy and strong was needed to go out, to run errands, to fetch materials. Jack immediately had a place in the team. And in return, Ben and Emily smuggled him food and he actually slept between sheets at night. The sheets were laid out on the settee in Ben's bedroom, but they were real.

Keeping Jack's existence from Mrs Mills, Cook, and the maids, Evans and Tillet, was an adventure Jack suspected Ben enjoyed more than he let on. Unlike his most recent adventure, even if the worst happened, no one was going to die.

Now the bookseller took the money but looked at Jack strangely. It was a well-to-do shop just off St Martin's Lane, and it didn't usually cater to boys like Jack.

"I'll get your change," he said, and withdrew into the back of the shop. Jack looked at the cover of the book he had just bought and pulled a face. A wild-eyed visage was engraved in gold on the cover and it bared large, square teeth at him. He couldn't read the title, but Emily had read it out loud as she wrote it down for him on an order slip to show to the man in the shop. *Theory and Practice of the Mayan Calendar*. He hoped it would be of use to her.

He glanced around him, bored. The shop was dim and the walls were lined with books that gave a rich, stuffy feel to the air. It was quiet and respectable – two things Jack wasn't used to. Outside, the street with its mid-morning throng looked much more inviting. Through the window, he ran a practised eye over the crowd.

Jack was far from being a confirmed thief. He had stolen things in his time because he had had to stay alive. He was glad that with the friendship of Emily and Ben, he had no need to steal any more. Still, old habits died hard. Just by looking at the sea of faces he could instantly tell who were the likely marks.

Then he frowned, because one face in particular had caught his attention. It belonged to a middle-aged man, pale and drawn and tired. He stumbled as he walked. Jack leaned closer to the glass to study him more carefully.

"Here you are." The bookseller came out from the back with a pile of change which he handed over.

Jack glanced at it casually – he couldn't read but he could count very quickly – and looked up. "Three shillings short," he said.

The bookseller sneered. "You think they'll believe you didn't take it?"

"Yes," Jack said calmly, with complete certainty. "They will." He held the man's gaze without blinking, and eventually the man flushed and looked away.

"I . . . I don't usually do the change," he said. He dug in his pocket for the missing three shillings. "That's usually my assistant, but he's not in today. Just didn't turn up. He's been tired for the last few days – must have caught something. . . Now what is it?"

Jack was staring at him. "Nothing," he said. "Thanks for the change, squire."

"Oh, get out of here," the man snapped. Jack turned and left.

Outside, he stood on tiptoes to search for the pale

man. He wasn't hard to find, as he hadn't got much further down the street. Jack set off after him out of curiosity. The man stumbled again as his legs buckled but somehow he found the strength to straighten up. A minute later he finally fell against someone else and went down, lifeless. There were gasps and shouts from the crowd, and by the time Jack got to him, he was surrounded by a group of men and women who were keeping a safe distance. They were drawn by tragedy but didn't want to get close to a corpse.

The man's face was sheet white and his dead eyes stared up at the sky.

"Give him air! Give him air!" A policeman had taken over and was shooing back the crowd of onlookers. Jack kept his distance from the copper out of old habits.

"Too late for that, mate," said someone. "He's a goner."

"The cholera's raging in Soho," said another.

"Nah, it ain't the cholera. You leaks from every hole with the cholera," said someone else gleefully. "This man ain't leakin'. He ain't got a drop left."

" . . .must be the Plague. . ."

"Nah, you swells up with that. . ."

". . .all over Whitechapel, too, people turning white as ghosts. . ."

". . .and Westminster. . ."

". . .St Giles. . ."

"Crikey," Jack muttered, and headed back to Bedford Square.

CHAPTER TEN

Jack made his way round to the back of the Coles' house. He didn't knock at the front door, because if he did, Mrs Mills was likely to answer it.

The housekeeper had reluctantly accepted the story that Emily had suggested and which Ben had told her: Harrison Cole and Edwin Sherwood were still in Mexico, and Ben had gone on ahead back to England. After all, why would Ben lie to her about something like that? The arrival of a ghost ship in the Port of London had been all over the news, but she hadn't put the two together, because who would? London was the busiest port in the world, and ships came and went all the time. Any one of them could have been Ben's.

She had even swallowed Ben's story about Harrison writing her a letter to explain everything, which he had then lost. But she would not allow a street child like Jack into the house. Even Ben's authority was limited in that area.

Instead, Jack climbed a drainpipe and tapped on Ben's window. A moment later Ben appeared and helped Jack inside.

"Just keeled over?" queried Ben later. The three of them were in Harrison's study. Like the rest of the house it was quiet, peaceful and spotless. The walls were lined with hundreds of leather-bound volumes. It reminded Jack of the bookseller's shop, but cleaner, and with a thick red carpet and well-polished furniture. Emily sat at Harrison's desk and was leafing through the book Jack had bought. Five or six other books from her father's small library were scattered around her. Ben and Jack were over in one corner while she worked.

"One minute staggering along, the next he's dead," Jack said. "And he ain't the first. I been hearing tales from all over. Even the shopkeeper's boy's got it."

Ben grimly held up that day's copy of *The Times*. "And the society pages are full of cancellations without explanation. It's as if the plague's in town, only there's no plague. No one wants to own up to it, because if they did, they'd have to explain why so many bodies are being found without any blood in them. And there's something else. Listen to this." He raised his voice. "Em? Em!"

Emily had been absorbed in her studies. With one finger she was following the text in the book Jack had bought; with the other she was doing the same with a book taken from the bookshelf behind her. She looked up.

"Listen," said Ben again. He opened up the newspaper and read from the third page. " 'The body of an unknown man was found floating in the Thames yesterday below Waterloo. . .' "

"Ain't nothing unusual about that," Jack commented.

Ben shot him a look and went back to the newspaper. " 'The man's heart is said to have been removed prior to his immersion. A doctor reported that his breastbone had been crudely hacked open with a sharp implement.' " He folded up the newspaper again and frowned at them both. "Sound familiar?" he asked.

"Blimey!" Jack said. "Usually when the heavies want someone dead, they hits him on the head and throws him in the river. They don't cut out his heart. . ."

Emily and Ben were both looking at him oddly.

"Ben's point is that this is how the Mayans sacrificed people, Jack," Emily said in a kindly way, and Jack felt foolish.

"Oh," he said. "You, um, think it's Sir Donald, then?"

"Well, it's never happened before as far as I know," Ben said simply. He turned to his sister. "How are you getting on, Em?"

Emily sighed and consulted her notes. "I've learned a great deal about Camazotz," she said, "but according to this book, well, if I understand the Mayan calendar properly, he seems to have disappeared about a thousand years ago. No one's heard of him since. What I don't

103

know is *why* he disappeared. What was he doing for a thousand years?"

"Living in a cave?" Jack suggested.

"For an entire millennium?" said Ben. "He could have got out sooner. If he wanted victims, there're plenty of people in Mexico. Or he could head north to the United States. What would keep him in a cave for a thousand years?"

"It's possible that Mexico's too small for him now," Emily said. "The Mayans ruled a mighty empire once. Now that it's fallen, maybe Camazotz wants to move on."

"I see," Ben murmured.

"I don't," Jack said.

"What's the greatest city in the world?" Ben asked him.

"London!" Jack replied proudly. And then, suddenly, he did see it. "Oh!"

"He's come to the heart of the empire," Emily went on. "He wants to take London. Then he can take the rest of the country. Then he can take India and Africa. . ."

"Still don't explain why he took a thousand years to get round to it," Jack pointed out.

"No, it doesn't," Ben agreed, "but we can worry about that later. For the moment, our empire is bigger than he ever dreamed of in the Yucatan. If he takes over, he could make us all vampires." He hung his head in thought, then looked up at them. "Em," he said, "you've been going through those books for days. Is there anything, even the slightest hint, about how we could fight him?"

Emily paused, then shook her head. "No," she answered quietly.

Ben bit his lip. "I didn't want to do this," he said, "but we've reached our limit. We have to tell someone else."

Jack burst out laughing. "Who was you planning on telling? You want to write to *The Times*? I'm sorry, Ben, but no one will believe you." He saw the pain in Ben's grey eyes, and immediately felt sorry for laughing.

"I know," Ben said. "I can try and *perhaps* no one will believe us. But if I don't try, I *know* no one will. We'll go to the police." He grinned suddenly and nudged Jack. "But look. We've a surprise for you."

Emily checked the coast was clear, then she and Ben hurried Jack upstairs to Ben's room. Jack stopped short at the sight of several sets of clothes lying on Ben's bed.

"Mrs Mills thought that because I've got so thin, she should have my suit taken in. I asked her to do the same with all my clothes," Ben explained. "We're about the same height. They should fit you now."

Jack's jaw dropped. He looked at the faces of his friends, smiling and eager to please, and suddenly he didn't know what to say. Two thoughts had immediately struck him. One was that, to be quite honest, his own clothes looked much more comfortable. The other was how nice it was to have friends.

He looked at Ben and Emily again, and saw their smiles wavering. They could see something was bothering him. Perhaps they thought he was too proud to accept charity. But Jack knew they weren't doing this out of pity. It was out of friendship, because they wanted him to be part of their world. So he smiled back. "Thank you, Ben. Maybe you should show me how to wear them, and then we can all go to the coppers."

In fact Jack came with them as far as the door of Bow Street police station. His conscience was clear but he was always uncomfortable close to the forces of law and order.

He leaned against the wall across the road with his hands in his pockets. It was coming up to lunch time, and the streets were busy. Horse-drawn cabs came clattering past; men and women hurried by on their daily business. Jack wondered how many would still be alive in a week. He shuddered. It was a frightening thought. What had Ben said? "It's as if the plague's in town." It *was* like the plague. There was something in London that was silent and invisible and deadly. How many lives had Sir Donald and his vampires claimed already?

A newspaper boy stood at the corner of the street, shouting out the headlines. Jack had never read a newspaper in his life and he looked away. Then he glanced back, because something had caught his attention. He listened more carefully.

"*Daily News!*" the boy shouted. "Break-in at British Museum! Priceless Mayan artefact stolen! Read all about it! *Daily News!*"

Jack wandered slowly over to the street corner and dug in his pocket. "How much?" he asked.

"Penny for you, squire," the boy said cheerfully. He filled his lungs and his shout of "*Daily News!*" made Jack take a step back.

Jack found a penny in his pocket and looked at it thoughtfully. Earlier that day he had handed over a pound for a book, of all things, but that was someone else's money. He had been given the penny as a reward for picking up a lady's handkerchief in the street, and returning it to her. It was his. Usually he would have spent it on food – that was what pennies were for. But he knew Ben and Emily would want to read the paper.

So he handed the penny over and returned to his place at the wall with a folded-up copy of the *Daily News*. He got there just as Emily and Ben were coming out of the police station.

He could see immediately that it had not gone well. Ben was pale and his jaw was clamped tight shut. Emily was red-faced and annoyed. Jack let them speak first.

"They . . . they. . ." stammered Emily.

"They didn't believe us," Ben said flatly. "They just laughed."

"And, and they told us. . ." Emily went on.

"They told us to go back to our mama!" Ben

exclaimed. Jack could see the anger seething beneath his calm demeanour.

"They acted as if we were little children. . ." said Emily.

"As if we were lying!" added Ben.

Jack winced. He had learned a long time ago that to say "I told you so" was never helpful.

"What can we do now?" Emily asked. "Who is going to believe us?"

"Um," said Jack. He brandished the newspaper. "Dunno if this will help. . ."

Ben took the paper curiously and unfurled it. His eyes scanned the headlines and he read them out loud. "'Prime Minister' . . . no. . . 'Ship lost at' . . . no. . ." Suddenly his eyes grew round. "Listen to this, Em. 'Break-in at British Museum. Priceless Mayan artefact stolen'. Here's what it says. 'Police are baffled by a break-in at the British Museum last night. All the signs are of forced entry. However, museum staff were slow to notice that there had been a robbery because at first everything seemed to be in place. It was only when the Curator of South American Artefacts, Professor Alfred Adensnap, arrived mid-morning that it was realized a robbery had occurred. The missing item was a small golden statue of a bat, brought back from Mexico by the explorer Edwin Sherwood.'"

Emily gasped. "Uncle Edwin's statue!"

Ben kept reading. "'In an unrelated incident, in what

is believed to be the most advanced case so far of the mysterious illness sweeping the capital, a museum guard was found dead at his post in a state of considerable exsanguination.'"

"Exsangy-what?" asked Jack.

"It means drained of blood," Ben told him. He slowly folded up the newspaper. "Unrelated, my foot! Sir Donald was after that statue." Another thought struck him. "And I remember him asking Uncle Edwin about it. He must have been finding out where it was."

Jack frowned. "What does he want it for?" he queried.

"I don't know," Ben replied frankly. "Perhaps Uncle Edwin could have told us."

"And p'raps this Professor Adensnap still can?" Jack suggested.

Ben blinked, then grinned and thumped Jack on the arm. "Em, Jack," he said. "I think we should visit Professor Adensnap."

CHAPTER ELEVEN

Although neither of them felt hungry, Emily pointed out that she and Ben ought to go home for lunch in order to avoid arousing Mrs Mills's suspicions. Jack, who was always hungry – and knew that his friends would smuggle food out to him – thought this was an excellent idea. So the three of them made their way back to Bedford Square.

Mrs Mills insisted on an hour's rest after eating, as she always did. But, by three o'clock, they were able to venture out again. After only a few minutes' walk they found themselves standing outside the British Museum.

Jack stared at the great building with round, astonished eyes. "This ain't a museum, it's a palace!" he declared.

The front of the museum was an immense facade, three storeys high, supported by powerful pillars that thrust up out of the ground. A wide flight of steps led up to the main entrance.

Emily and Ben smiled at each other and Ben patted Jack on the back. "The only kings and queens here are long dead," he said. "You get used to it. Come on."

Ben and Emily went up the steps as if they lived there. They had been to the museum many times before, usually with their father. The doorman recognized them and touched the brim of his hat as they passed. "Good afternoon, Master Cole, Miss Cole," he said.

Inside, the museum seemed just as grand. Jack gazed about him in awe. The ceiling seemed about half a mile above him. The vast stone corridors and hallways echoed softly with the passing feet of visitors and a hundred murmured conversations. This was a place where you *had* to be quiet. Noise was just out of the question.

Ben led the way up a flight of wide stone stairs and along a gallery. A side door led them into some passages, away from the usual haunts of the public. Ben had to ask the way, but they eventually reached the office of Professor Adensnap.

"Come in!" called a quavering voice in response to their knock on the door. Ben opened the door and the three of them filed in.

Professor Adensnap was sitting behind his desk, quill pen in one hand. He had a ring of snowy white hair around the crown of his otherwise bald head, and a pair of spectacles perched on the end of his nose. They fell off when he looked up to see his visitors. He immediately put them back on again, but the friends soon learnt that they would fall off every minute or so – and he rarely looked through them anyway.

"Ah!" he said when he saw his three visitors. He had a dry, breathy voice that shook slightly. "I thought you might be the police again. More of those tedious questions. But, no. A nice change. Lost your parents, have you? I can call someone. . ."

Ben had to interrupt. "We came to see *you*, Professor Adensnap," he said.

"Came to see *me*? Bless me! I'm touched. Honoured. Privileged. Delighted! Young minds are so important. So important. Got to reach 'em early. Come in, come in. Sit down, um, somewhere."

The office was lined with bookcases and drawers. A dim yellow light came through one grimy window that looked out on to the museum's Great Court. Every surface was taken up with masses of books and printed papers and a layer of dust. A map of South America hung askew behind the door.

Professor Adensnap came round his desk and swept a pile of manuscripts off a settee in one corner. It was just big enough to take the three friends if they squeezed together. Jack and Ben sat at either end with Emily pressed uncomfortably between them.

"Not really one for entertaining youngsters," Adensnap said apologetically. "I'd offer you a sherry if you were a bit older. Could probably manage some tea. . ."

Ben took the lead again. He leaned forward with his elbows on his knees. "Professor, my name is Benedict Cole. This is my sister, Emily, and—"

"Cole? Cole?" Adensnap's face lit up. "Any relation to Harrison Cole? As in Cole and Sherwood?"

"He. . ." Ben dried up, and he and Emily exchanged a glance.

Jack took over. "He's their father, Professor," he said.

"Harrison Cole's children? Bless me! How wonderful. Very clever chap, your father. Done some valuable work. Heard he was off to Mexico."

"He's still there," Jack added, to forestall another awkward silence.

"Marvellous, marvellous," Adensnap said. "Well, Harrison Cole's children, what can I do for you?"

"We read about the theft of the statue in the newspaper, Professor," Emily told him. "We were very sorry to hear about it. Edwin Sherwood was our godfather."

Adensnap's face clouded. "Yes, indeed. Sorry doesn't begin to cover it. Look at this." He crossed over to one side of the office and pushed aside a pile of books. A small metal safe stood against the wall, its door hanging from one hinge. "See that? Cost a good deal of money, that did. Guaranteed security, they said. And some fella comes in off the street and opens it like it was made of tin. See these marks, here? If I didn't know better, I'd say the chap tore it open with his bare hands."

"We're very interested in that statue, sir," said Ben. "I wondered if you could tell us about it?"

"Tell you? Tell you?" Adensnap's good humour returned at once. "Delighted! Not enough interest in the pre-Colombian civilizations, you know. Not nearly enough. It's all Greeks and Romans. Expect you get that coming out of your ears at school. But those chappies in South America weren't stupid, you know. Not stupid at all. Ghastly religions, unbelievably bloodthirsty. Wouldn't want your daughter to marry one. But not stupid."

"And the statue, sir?" Ben prodded gently.

"Ah, yes, the statue. A great loss. Only consolation is that the chap will find it impossible to sell. One of a kind, y'know. Well, unless you agree with Sherwood's theory that it was made by the same craftsman as Dampierre's piece. . ."

There was only one way to listen to Adensnap. You had to let him ramble, and eventually he would reach the point.

He rummaged again, and found a black ink drawing of the bat statue which he showed them. The bat's wings were outstretched, as if it was about to embrace something. Or to pounce.

"Brought back to this country by your godfather," he said. "Not much known about it, because we know so little about the Mayan language. Your own father is doing sterling work in that area, y'know."

"But it definitely had something to do with Camazotz?" Emily asked.

"Eh? Camazotz? Oh, yes, yes. No question about that. Camazotz. Nastiest of a bunch of nasty gods. Hah!"

"So what's the statue for?" inquired Jack. "Decoration?"

Adensnap seemed to approve of this query. "Good question, young man," he said. "Good question. The Mayans were very fond of symbols. As below, so above, and all that. Probably the statue had a symbolic purpose. Use it to do something on earth, and you get the same effect in the world beyond," the professor explained. "We don't know what the statue was for, but it's likely it would have done something to enhance Camazotz's power."

This time there was a much longer pause while the friends took this in. Adensnap sat back in his chair and studied them with an intelligent gleam in his eye. He still looked old, but suddenly he didn't sound half as daft and vague. "Now," he said, "what's all this to you?"

Jack, Ben and Emily looked at each other. The memory of the police station was still fresh in their minds, and Emily and Ben didn't want to make fools of themselves twice in one day.

So Jack spoke. "We think this Camazotz is here in London today," he said. "We think it was him as took the statue. We know people are dying out there and we think he's to blame. Ben here saw him in action in Mexico, and now he's in London."

Adensnap raised his eyebrows. "The last we heard of Camazotz was a thousand years ago," he said mildly. "I doubt your friend saw him recently." It was impossible to tell from his tone whether he was amused, about to explode in anger, or just incredulous. Ben sensed he was neither believing nor disbelieving. He was hitting the ball back into their court. Whether the professor believed or not after that would depend on how they responded.

It wasn't much, but it was more than the police had given them. And that thin thread of hope gave Ben confidence to speak. "It's an incredible story, sir," he said. "But did you read in the papers, a week ago, about a ghost ship putting in at the docks?"

"I did," confirmed Adensnap.

"Well, I was on it," Ben said flatly. "And you've read about this strange new illness going around?"

"I have. Cholera, they say, which convinces no one who has encountered the real thing for a second. More like a very pernicious form of anaemia. Had a great aunt once with something very similar. Are you involved in that too, Master Cole?"

Ben ignored the question. "And last night, *The Times* says, a man was found in the Thames with his heart cut out. A very Mayan practice, as you'll be aware, sir."

Adensnap just looked at him, and Ben swallowed.

"Shall . . . shall I just tell my story, sir?" he suggested nervously.

Adensnap leaned forward. "I think that would be an excellent idea."

CHAPTER TWELVE

Professor Adensnap listened intently as Ben related the story he had already told Jack and Emily; from the discovery of the cave and the bats in Mexico, to his return to London. At one point the professor stood slowly and crossed to the window. With his hands behind his back, he stared out at the Great Court through the smeared glass.

Finally, Ben reached the point where the ship arrived in London and Jack helped him get home. He mentioned Emily's further researches and then trailed off into silence. The three friends waited with bated breath.

Adensnap slowly returned to his seat. He leaned back in it and gazed at them out of clear blue eyes. His glasses fell off again. "Cole and Sherwood, both dead," he said quietly. "My deepest commiserations. A tragedy for *you*, and an irreplaceable loss to the field."

"But, do you believe us, Professor?" Emily asked hesitantly. "About, um, everything else Ben told you?"

"My dear girl, I am trying hard *not* to," he said. "Stand up, Master Cole."

Ben glanced at Jack and Emily, then did as he was told.

"Turn around. Sit down," Adensnap instructed. Ben obeyed all these directions with a baffled look on his face.

"This young man," said Adensnap, waving a hand at Jack, "is naturally thin and always has been. He grew up that way. You can tell from the way his skin sits comfortably on his bones. I doubt he has ever had an ounce of surplus weight on him in his life."

"That's true," Jack muttered.

"You, on the other hand, were once comfortably well fed," the professor told Ben. "Now your bones stick out and your clothes hang off you, despite your tailor's best efforts. So, you have certainly starved recently. Was it on a long sea voyage? I couldn't say. But there is clearly something in your tale that could be true, according to the available evidence."

He leaned back and steepled his fingers. "Evidence, evidence! The hallmark of the scientific method! You mentioned the ship, and you mentioned this illness that isn't cholera. All of it evidence, not necessarily pointing to the same conclusion, but still worthy of consideration."

"Then why didn't the police listen?" demanded Ben. "I said exactly the same thing to them."

Adensnap snorted. "My dear boy, try to compare like with like. The police are here to catch criminals. Let every man stick to his speciality, I say, and my speciality is the Mayan Empire. Let me tell you what *I* know, and then perhaps you'll see why I don't rush to embrace your story.

"Now, I know about Camazotz, of course. His name turns up everywhere in Mayan mythology. According to legend, his bloodlust brought about the downfall of the Mayan civilization. As he became more widely worshipped and more powerful, he demanded more blood sacrifices. Meanwhile, his vampires were feeding off the still-human Mayans. Eventually there weren't enough humans left to feed all the vampires and sustain Camazotz."

The professor had been talking as if it were all true. Now he held up a finger to stop any of the friends from interrupting. "That is the *legend*," he said. "The *legend* also talks about the rebel priesthood of the rain and lightning god, Chac. They somehow instigated a rebellion and forced Camazotz, together with his remaining vampire followers, into hibernation for a millennium. I concede that according to our understanding of Mayan dates, this would have been roughly one thousand years ago – about the end of the classic period of the Mayan Empire – which would mean he's due to wake up any time now. But that still doesn't mean I believe you.

"You see, like most modern scholars, I have always assumed Camazotz was just a particularly nasty human leader. Look at Julius Caesar and Ivan the Terrible! Both purely human, both with some quite filthy habits. And the banishment? Well, no tyrant ever lasts. Annoy enough people and one of them will hit you on the head. It's been like that since the dawn of time and that's how it will always be. The legend talks of Camazotz going to sleep – we assume he was killed, which for the Mayans was pretty much the same thing.

"You see, my young friends, my version of events satisfies all the facts and gives us the reassurance that Camazotz was dead and buried a long time ago. Now you're asking me to overturn convictions I've had all my life, in a matter of minutes. It won't be easy."

"All *my* life, I'd never believed in demons, sir," Ben said, "until a few months ago."

Adensnap's eyes twinkled. "With respect, dear boy, my life has been somewhat longer than yours."

"You wanted evidence," Ben said. "Well, surely everything I've told you ties in with what you've been telling us?"

"Oh, it does," Adensnap said mildly and sighed. "That's the problem. You see, if you're right, then certain other things must surely follow that are quite terrifying to contemplate. That is why I told your dear sister that I was trying *not* to believe. If you really found Camazotz in a cave where he had lain for a millennium, and if he really awoke and possessed Sir Donald Finlay and came back here to London – why, he is growing more powerful day by day, and soon we will face exactly the same problems as the Ancient Mayans. And quite possibly, exactly the same fate!

"Camazotz's vampire followers can turn humans into vampires like themselves – and thus they create more servants for their god. Now, say that one vampire creates one other in a day. You have two vampires. The next day, they each create another. Now you have four. The next day . . . and so on. Eight vampires. Sixteen vampires. Thirty-two vampires. By the end of the week, one hundred and twenty-eight vampires! And that is starting with just one – and assuming that they each create only one vampire a day. In fact, we are starting with over a hundred, you say, and we have no idea how quickly they work. London could be overrun in no time at all. *That* is why I so desperately want you to be wrong."

He paused, to let the three friends take in the image of a London overrun by a demon god and his vampire servants.

"Still, a good scientist never runs from the facts," Professor Adensnap continued. "Your story fits with certain details that you could not have known beforehand. Let us investigate something else that I doubt you already knew."

He knelt down and rummaged through yet another pile of books. Finally he found what he was looking for

– a large black box file. He slammed it down on the desk and a cloud of dust filled the room.

Adensnap rested his hands on the file without opening it, and waited for them to stop sneezing. "You mentioned these blood roses around the cave," he said. "Describe them again."

Ben screwed up his face to remember. "They were like ordinary garden roses, but a very deep scarlet. Their scent was so sickly sweet and strong that it made me feel ill. And their thorns were very sharp – and curved, like . . . like fangs."

"Like these?" asked Adensnap, as he opened the file. Ben, Jack and Emily crowded round to look. On top of a pile of papers inside the file was a tattered, yellowing sheet of parchment.

In one corner of the parchment someone had drawn a cluster of flowers, surrounded by cruel-looking thorns shaped not unlike the teeth of vampire bats. Their petals had faded to a dull crimson but must once have been a brilliant red. In the corner opposite the flowers, small, black bat shapes swirled up from what was clearly the opening of a cave, and they flew up to surround a fanged, snarling face drawn in black and red.

In between the pictures, every square inch of parchment was covered with cramped handwriting and the curved, organic shapes of Mayan hieroglyphs.

"Yes!" Ben exclaimed. "That's them! Blood roses!"

"Oh, my goodness," Adensnap murmured. More

loudly, he went on, "The blood rose and Camazotz are always closely associated in the mythology." He patted the manuscript. "This was all copied on to the parchment by a Spanish missionary in the sixteenth century. These lines, here, are the missionary's notes. See..." He pointed at a small line of recognizable handwriting in Spanish. "He says: 'The Mayan priest, Pokom, who showed me these designs said they were the ritual used by his forefathers to banish the plague of Camazotz from the land'. And the rose seems to be involved. Can we assume it is a bane of some kind, poisonous to vampires? Perhaps used in this ritual? It could be that the priests of Chac planted it all around Camazotz's cave to keep him in. So when Sir Donald and his men cut the roses away..." Adensnap slumped and rested his head in his hand. "Dear Lord. Can it really be so? Can the legends be true?"

Emily tentatively put her hand on his shoulder. "I know how terrible it is, sir, but it *is* true."

"But it's not terrible!" Ben put in suddenly. Everyone looked at him, and he pointed at the parchment. "You said it yourself, sir. This is a ritual to banish Camazotz!" Emily and Jack suddenly felt a surge of hope.

"Which," Adensnap said sadly, "we can't read. It's all in Mayan hieroglyphs – which nobody has yet been able to translate."

Ben suddenly grabbed hold of the professor's hand and pumped it up and down. "Well, thank you, sir," he said. "Thank you, that's been most helpful. Most helpful."

"Really?" Adensnap looked surprised. "Well, glad I could help. . ."

"Ben?" asked Emily, looking confused. "What are you talking about?"

"No time, no time!" Ben said excitedly. For a moment he almost sounded like Adensnap himself. "We'll be back, sir, and we'll bring something immensely helpful with us. Come on, you two! Come on!"

And he ushered Emily and Jack back out into the corridor and shut the door behind them, while Adensnap was still asking what he meant.

Ben wouldn't say anything until they were out of the museum.

"What's got into you, Ben?" Jack demanded as they hurried down the great steps towards the gates.

Ben stopped and turned to Jack and Emily. His face was shining. "I didn't want to tell Professor Adensnap in case I'm wrong, but . . . well. . ."

"*Yes?*" Jack and Emily prompted together.

"He said no one can read Mayan hieroglyphs. Wrong!" Ben looked even more excited than the professor had. "Father could! He told me he had done a translation. Still sketchy, he said, but there might be enough for us to work from. It will be in his notebooks."

Jack heaved a sigh. He really didn't want to be the one to point out the obvious problem – that Ben's father was *dead* – but it looked like he was going to have to.

Then suddenly, Emily lit up too. "So if we can get those notebooks –" she began.

"Yes! *Yes!*" Ben agreed.

"But ain't they back in Mexico?" Jack asked slowly. He said it that way because if they weren't in Mexico, there was only one other place they were likely to be. Frankly, Jack hoped they were still in Mexico.

He had guessed correctly. Ben calmed down and swallowed nervously. "Um, no," he said. "They would have been brought back with all the other expedition material. . ."

"I see," Jack said.

So did Emily. "Oh, no," she said, after a long pause. "You mean, they'll be at *Sir Donald's house*?"

"Yes," said Ben, slowly. "Which is probably where Sir Donald is, too. And you heard what the professor said about how quickly the number of vampires could increase. We have to stop Sir Donald as soon as we can – which means we have to go to his house and get Father's notebooks, before it's too late."

CHAPTER THIRTEEN

Sir Donald Finlay's home was a mansion on the edge of Mayfair, to the west of London. Taking a hansom cab there was a novel experience for Jack, who was more used to hitching a free lift on the back of a cart. The cab was a two-wheeled carriage, open at the front. The seat was just large enough for the three friends to sit comfortably, side by side. A small roof kept off any rain that might have fallen from above or behind, but would have been useless if the rain had come from the front. Fortunately, on that May afternoon, it wasn't raining.

The driver sat high up behind the cab. Jack wasn't sure he liked having someone close by, unseen, who could hear every word they said. So he didn't say anything until they got out of the cab in Mayfair and made their way to Sir Donald's residence.

"That's the house?" Jack asked. Like many other squares in London, this one had a small garden in the middle where they could lurk in the bushes without being seen. The houses here were larger and grander than the Coles' own. The house in Bedford Square was terraced. These were all massive, monumental mansions, standing in their own grounds. Each one was separated from the next by a narrow alleyway. At the back would be the gardens, surrounded by a high wall. At the front, steps from the front door led right down to the street.

Three rows of sash windows gazed blankly at them, with smaller casement windows set into the slope of the roof. The front of the house was dominated by a vast, pillared porch.

"That's the one," Ben confirmed. "Emily and I have both been here often enough."

"We don't know that Sir Donald is in there, Ben," Emily pointed out. "In Sir Donald's form, Camazotz could go anywhere."

"Yes," Ben agreed. "But he would probably want somewhere to sleep during the day – and he might as well make use of this place."

"What time is it?" Jack asked.

Ben checked his pocket watch. "Four o'clock," he replied. "We have plenty of daylight left."

"And Sir Donald and his vampires can't stand daylight, right?" Jack queried nervously.

"I think it's only direct sunlight that actually hurts them," Ben told him. "In Mexico, Sir Donald and the bats seemed to cope well with the ordinary daylight – it was the sunbeams they couldn't stand. But it was definitely the night time when they were most … active," he finished, and shuddered at the memory.

"So, while it's daytime, let's hope Sir Donald – and any of his vampires that are in there with him – are all sleeping soundly," said Emily with feeling.

"Well, someone's awake, look," Jack muttered, pointing at the house.

The front door had opened a crack. There was a pause, and then a young woman in a maid's cap and apron sidled out. She glanced from side to side, then gently shut the door and tiptoed down the steps into the sunlight. As soon as she reached the street, she started to hurry away.

"Well, she's still human," Ben murmured, when it was clear that the sunlight was doing the maid no harm at all. He went back to watching the house.

"Wait here," Emily said, and she ran off after the maid. The boys glanced at each other in surprise, then followed her.

By the time they reached Emily, she had caught up with the woman. She was young, probably no more than two or three years older than Emily.

"…up all night," she was saying to Emily, "a-and asleep all day. I never seed him since he got back, just that creepy butler, Mr Brown, makin' me do all the errands, now the staff is gone. . ."

"That's odd – I thought Mr Rivers was Sir Donald's butler," Emily put in.

"Rivers retired shortly before the expedition left," Ben told her. "I met Mr Brown once. He seemed a friendly type. So Sir Donald *is* back, then?" Ben asked the maid, eager for confirmation. "He *has* returned?"

She gave him a strange look. "Back a week ago, sir. And straight ways, the other staff start leavin' – or disappearin' anyway. They never says goodbye, which I thought was odd, they just ain't there in the mornin'. It's all very strange and I tell you, frankly, miss, I don't like it a bit," she said, turning back to Emily. "When I got to work this mornin'," she went on, "there was just me! Me and Mr Brown! And you're right about 'im – he were such a nice gent, once. But now he's grim and cold, and he creeps about so as to come upon me sudden like when I'm not expecting it – as if he's trying to catch me doing something wrong. And then today, he comes and tells me how I'm wanted in the cellar – where, usually, none of us are ever allowed to go any more. And I can't help wondering if the rest of the staff were 'wanted in the cellar' too! And so I'm not taking any chances. It used to be a happy house, but now it's a terrible place and I'm gettin' out while I can."

"It sounds horrible," Emily agreed. "I wonder . . . um . . . could I take your cap? And your apron?"

"I beg your pardon, miss?" the woman asked, surprised.

"Your cap and apron?" Emily repeated. "Please?" She dug into her purse and held out some pennies.

"Look, I'll buy them off you. It's not much, but—"

"Miss," the woman said, "this is me uniform, like. Beggin' your pardon, but if I sells these, how am I goin' to get a new position?"

Emily tipped the entire contents of her purse into the maid's hand. "Seven shillings and . . . thruppence," she said. "I'm afraid it's all I have."

The maid was staring at the small fortune. It would buy a new cap and apron, and feed her for several days as well. She beamed. "Of course you can have 'em, miss! Yours for the takin'." She handed over the garments, took the money and set off with a spring in her step.

"Em," Ben said slowly, "what are you doing?"

Emily flourished the apron proudly. "How hard can it be?" she demanded. "I've watched Mrs Mills often enough. I'm going to take that girl's job!"

Ben gasped. "No!" he exclaimed. "No! It's too dangerous!"

"And how else do you plan to get into the house?" Emily asked him. "No one notices the servants. It will be a perfect disguise! I'll be able to look around and find Father's notebooks."

"But. . ." Ben argued. "It would be safer if I went instead."

"You can't," Emily replied calmly. "You've met this new butler, Mr Brown. He might recognize you. And there's no reason why he'd let Jack into the house. Ben, I have to be the one who does this."

Ben sighed in defeat and gave his sister a hug. "Go to the tradesman's door," he told her. "You know what Mrs Mills is like when they come to the front."

"Of course," she agreed – and smiled and hugged Ben in return. "Go back to the bushes. I'll try not to be long." And, clutching the cap and apron, Emily turned and walked bravely up to the house.

CHAPTER FOURTEEN

The tradesman's entrance was round the back. The alley between the buildings was narrow and dark, and the house towered over Emily. For a moment sheer terror threatened to overwhelm her and she was tempted to run back to the boys hiding in the shrubbery, but she gritted her teeth, clenched her fists and kept walking.

The door she wanted was down a short flight of steps. She rang the bell, then stepped back and waited.

After a little while it opened. Inside was a dark, gloomy passage, and for a moment Emily could have sworn that the door had opened of its own accord, but then a human figure loomed out of the dark. He wore a butler's black morning coat and Emily breathed a sigh of relief – it wasn't Sir Donald.

The butler was tall and thin with grey hair and sunken eyes. The corners of his mouth were down-turned, like the hands of a clock that always said twenty minutes to four. He looked down his nose at her. "Yes?" There was a faint hint of Scots in his tone, but it lacked any kind of warmth.

Emily took a deep breath. "Beg your pardon, sir," she said. "But I wondered if you might have a vacancy for a maid? I'm in need of employment, you see."

He stared down at her for a few moments. Then, without another word, he stepped back from the door and indicated that she should enter. She hesitated just a moment, knowing that beyond this point she would be truly alone. But she could think of no other way to retrieve her father's work, and so she stepped into the gloom.

The butler shut the door behind her, and what little light there was vanished. He was just a dark shape, his white shirt a pale blur in the shadows. And then Emily bit back a gasp, because where his eyes were she could have sworn she saw a red gleam.

The butler locked the door, and Emily's heart pounded so hard, she was sure he would hear it. She knew that, whatever he was, she was trapped in here with him.

He walked past her. "This way," he said and led her into the servants' parlour, which was dimly lit by an oil lamp. He sat down at the table and held out his hand. "Your references?" he demanded.

References! Emily cursed herself. Of course, every servant in the city had references from their previous employers. She made a show of searching her pockets, then looked up at the butler in dismay. "Oh, sir, I must have dropped them!" she declared.

He held her gaze for a moment and Emily glimpsed that red gleam in his eyes again. It wasn't the whites of his eyes that were red – like someone who was tired or had been crying. The red glow lurked deep inside the pupils in a way that Emily found very disturbing.

"Clumsy," he remarked. "But we can send for some more." He pulled a notebook and pencil from his coat. "What is your name?"

"Emily Cole," she said immediately. And even as she was saying it, she realized her mistake and hurriedly added, "-man. Emily Coleman."

He wrote this down. "Who was your last employer, Coleman?"

Even though it was not her real surname, for a moment Emily was at a complete loss. She had never been addressed in such a way. Never. This was what it was like to be a servant.

"Mr. . ." she said, thinking furiously. "Benedict. Jack. Of . . . Russell Square."

He wrote without looking up. "Mr Benedict Jack of Russell Square. You are very well spoken for a maid, Coleman."

At this he did look up. There was an air of faint challenge in his tone and his eyes seemed to bore into her soul.

"Mr Jack insisted, sir," Emily replied. And then, as inspiration struck her, she added, "I was in charge of the children of the house, and he didn't want them learning to speak like a . . . like a servant."

"I see." Scribble, scribble. He looked up again. "There are no children in this house, Coleman."

"Um, yes, sir," Emily said. "I mean, no, sir."

"And, in fact, now Bennet has deserted us, there are no other staff either, apart from myself. My name is Mr Brown."

Emily tried to look surprised. "No other staff at all, sir?"

"There is only one resident. Our Master, Sir Donald Finlay. He likes solitude."

"But in a big house like this—" Emily began.

"Most of the rooms are closed permanently. The Master does not entertain visitors. He prefers to rest during the day and he is awake at night. Your duties will be to maintain the rooms that he does use. You will also run those errands that require someone to leave the house during the hours of daylight."

He hadn't actually said so, but Emily had the impression that the job was hers. "Very good, sir," she responded.

Mr Brown nodded and rose in one fluid movement. Emily took a step back. She had forgotten just how tall he was, until he stood over her.

"I had best show you the house," he said, picking up the lamp and moving it to the door.

Emily's heart quickened as she followed him up a narrow staircase and into the hallway. She remembered it from her earlier visits, when Sir Donald had still been human and a friend. The well of the hallway extended all the way up through the house to the attic. A grand flight of stairs swept upwards to each floor, and all the main rooms of the house opened off the central stairwell. The door they had come through, from the basement, was in the hall's far right corner. In the middle of the opposite wall, Emily saw the imposing front door, flanked by two large windows which were covered with heavy curtains. One of these curtains was caught up, so that a stray sunbeam had found its way into the hall. Emily watched as Mr Brown carefully picked his way around the patch of sunlight, and released the curtain so that his lamp became the only light source.

In the lamp's dim glow, Emily gazed around. The oak-panelled walls and landings were lined with stuffed animals – birds, mammals, creatures she didn't recognize – all the relics of Sir Donald's career as a biologist.

"Outside the servants' quarters and the basement, you are not to enter any room in the house without instructions from myself," Mr Brown said. "The only rooms that will concern you are here." He pointed at two doors in the left-hand wall of the hall. "The study. The withdrawing room." Then he turned and pointed to a small door set into the panelling of the right-hand wall, next to a large grandfather clock. "That door will take you to the cellar, which is strictly out of bounds. You will never have cause to enter there, unless specifically summoned. And finally –" he turned to the last door in the right wall – "the dining room. Come with me, Coleman."

The dining room was lined with the same thick, dark panelling as the hall. There was one large window that looked out towards the front of the house. A massive table took up most of the space. A cloth had been spread over it, on which silverware was laid out neatly.

Mr Brown looked sternly at Emily. "Your predecessor left this task unfinished," he said. "I suggest you carry on with it." He gave a faint, mocking bow, and backed into the hall, pulling the door shut behind him. After a moment, Emily heard his footsteps dying away.

She immediately hurried to the window. The curtains were not closed in here and she looked out into the square. She could see the bush where the boys should have been hiding and thought she could just make out their caps behind the leaves, but she wasn't sure if they could see her. She waved anyway. Then she turned back to the room, biting her lip thoughtfully.

She had no watch and no idea how long she had been in the house. It felt like for ever, but it was probably no more than ten minutes. She slipped off her coat, tied the apron round her waist and picked up a knife. She had never cleaned silver before, but she had often seen Evans, the maid, polish silver at home, so she knew how to do it. Just in case Mr Brown came back to inspect her progress, she decided to clean ten knives and ten forks. Then, if all was still clear, she would start her search.

According to the carriage clock on the mantelpiece, it took another ten minutes to get the cutlery to a satisfactory shine. There was no sign of Mr Brown, so she put her coat back on – in case she needed to leave hastily – tiptoed to the door and opened it cautiously. At least the last maid had kept the hinges oiled – it didn't creak. She slid out into the hall and hurried across to the room Mr Brown had called the study.

Nervously, Emily pushed the door open and peeped inside. The study was larger and tidier than her father's at home, but like the rest of Sir Donald's house, it felt dry and lifeless. Tall, glass-fronted bookcases stretched to the ceiling and a massive, mahogany desk with a green leather top sat in the middle of the room.

She crossed quickly to the desk and realized with delight that it was just as Ben had suspected – all the expedition's books and paperwork had come back from Mexico with Sir Donald and then been delivered to his house. The desktop was strewn with books and papers relating to the expedition's work in the Yucatan. Clearly Sir Donald had been examining the information that the explorers had collected.

Hurriedly, Emily sorted through the papers, searching for her father's familiar handwriting. Finding no sign of it, she opened the desk drawers as quickly and quietly as possible. She found letters and ledgers and folders, but none of her father's notebooks – until she pulled open the last drawer.

Inside was a whole stack of Harrison Cole's notebooks that someone had carefully bound together with string. She knew how her father worked – the books would be full of random scribbles and notes, but Harrison always wrote out a top copy in his journal to summarize everything he had learned. It was this journal that Emily needed to find.

She pulled the string off the pile and opened the first book. It was a leather volume that she herself had given her father for his birthday, shortly before the expedition left. Gold lettering on the cover said, "Journal of Harrison Cole". She turned to the first entry and her eyes misted at the sight of her father's writing: *11 November. Set off. Poor E still ill with fever so no chance of bringing her. B very excited. . .*

"Oh, Father," Emily whispered. She flicked further through the book, to make sure it held the right information, and then, to her horror, the study door started to open!

For a moment the world seemed to stand still while Emily's mind raced. She knew she had only a moment to conceal the journal before Mr Brown caught her. She stuffed the diary into her apron pocket and slid the drawer shut, just as the butler walked in and looked around.

His gaze fell on Emily almost immediately. Then she saw his eyes flicker briefly to the papers on the desk and return to rest on her again. She stepped away, not taking her eyes off him for a moment.

Mr Brown's face remained expressionless. "You have been very disobedient, Coleman," he said calmly.

"I-I'm sorry, sir," Emily stammered. "I was curious. I was just looking. I'll leave now, sir, if that's what you want. I'll not make any further –"

She gasped – because Mr Brown was finally smiling. The corners of his mouth crept up, and up, and up. And then his lips parted to reveal teeth – unnaturally white, sharp, perfect teeth. He ran his tongue over his pointed canines and his eyes shone with a red light.

"We will see what the Master says," he hissed.

CHAPTER FIFTEEN

Jack had learned to be patient long ago. He thought that Ben would have learned too, stuck in hiding on an Atlantic ship for weeks on end. But if Ben had ever learned, he had forgotten. He paced to and fro, back and forth, always shooting glances across the road at Sir Donald's house.

The sun had moved right across the sky and was casting a red glow on the front of the house. Before long it would be sunset.

Ben pulled his watch out of his coat pocket. It was close to nine o'clock. "She's been gone nearly five hours," he said.

They were quiet for a moment.

"Y'know, it's a big house," Jack pointed out. "It could take her a long time to—"

"I know!" Ben snapped. "But *five hours*? And sunset soon. You heard what the maid said – *he* wakes up at night." Ben looked uncomfortable, as if he was swallowing a pill. "Jack . . . I really need to ask you something."

"Yes?"

"Well, have you ever. . . What I mean is, er. . ."

Jack waited.

"Jack," Ben burst out, "I know you've stolen things in your time and you're not proud of it and, well, look, have you ever broken into a house?"

Jack blinked. "Um," he said. "Well, nearly, once. I ain't no expert."

Ben managed a weak smile. "That's still more than I have, unless you count my own house, the day we met."

"Uh, yeah. That was the once, actually," Jack admitted.

"Oh." Ben paused. "Well, I think we need to go in and find Emily."

"We might just disturb her," Jack began.

But Ben was shaking his head. "She's had five hours. And remember, she doesn't have to pretend, once she finds it. She could stuff it into her pocket and run for the front door. Vampires couldn't follow her into the sun." He looked over at the house. "No, Jack. They've caught her. I'm sure of it."

Or worse, Jack thought, but he had the sense not to say it out loud.

Ben forced a brave smile. "So, how do you think we should try and get in?" he asked. "What do you suggest?"

Jack thought about it. "I suggest we don't go to the front door," he said finally. "We goes in round the back."

Sir Donald's garden was surrounded by a tall brick wall. Jack put his hands together and boosted Ben up to sit on top of it. Then Ben reached down and helped Jack clamber up. They swung their legs over and dropped down.

They were in the bushes at the end of the garden, so they peered through the leaves at the house. They saw a neat lawn with a pond in the middle. French windows appeared to lead into a conservatory, and a first-floor balcony ran the length of the back of the house.

"You been here before," Jack whispered. "Where they going to keep a prisoner?"

Ben stared helplessly at the house. "I don't know. There're so many rooms. If we each took half of the house. . ."

"No," Jack said immediately. "No. We stick together, Ben."

Ben looked grateful that his idea had been dismissed. "Well, we can start at the bottom and work up," he suggested, "or start at the top and work down."

"Top down," Jack said. "That way, we gets closer and closer to the front door and the way out, 'stead of further and further away."

"Right. So, how do we get in?" Ben queried. He pointed at the french windows. "Through there?"

"No. . ." Jack replied thoughtfully. "We climbs up that pipe, and we goes through that window up there. See?" He was pointing at a drainpipe that ran up the side of the house, past the balcony. Ben could see that one of the windows on to the balcony was ajar. "That will get us to the first landing," Jack went on. "But first, we got to get across the lawn."

The boys looked at the stretch of grass between them and the house. It was only about thirty yards, but it was in full view of half the windows.

"If we was sensible, we'd wait till dark. . ." Jack muttered.

"No," Ben said firmly. "Better to go while it's still light, and hope Sir Donald and his vampires are asleep."

"Then we go now," Jack said decisively and patted Ben on the back. "Come on."

They scurried at a half-crouch across the lawn. The thirty yards seemed to take for ever. They reached the house with their hearts pounding, and pressed themselves against the wall. Jack reckoned vampires would react to two young intruders the same way as humans – with a hue and cry. All was quiet. They hadn't been seen.

He wrapped his arms and legs around the drainpipe, and shinned up. The pipe passed close to the balcony and Jack had to reach over to get a grip on the balustrade. He stretched out a leg until he felt stonework under his toes, then he let go of the pipe and pulled himself over.

When he looked back down, Ben was still on the ground, squinting up after him. He looked nervous, and Jack made an encouraging "come on" gesture. Ben swallowed and grasped the pipe in his hands. He squeezed it with his knees and followed clumsily after Jack.

Ben almost made it, but at the last minute his foot slipped and he fell forward. His chest thumped against the balustrade and he gasped in pain. Jack lunged over and grabbed him just in time to heave him over the balustrade, on to the balcony.

The boys didn't say anything; it was too dangerous. Jack glared, Ben sucked in his cheeks and looked sorry. Then Jack turned to the open window he had spotted from the ground. A moment later, they were inside the house.

It was quiet and dark. There was just enough light from the window for the boys to see bulky white shapes around them. They were in a bedroom, its walls lined with portraits of animals. Sheets covered the furniture. The room had presumably been put into storage when Sir Donald set off for Mexico. What came back in Sir Donald's place had had no interest in opening up the house again.

Emily was obviously not there, so they tiptoed to the door. A mighty creak made them freeze. They glanced at each other. It was Jack's turn to look apologetic as he slowly lifted his foot away from the floorboard. There was a quieter creak as the board relaxed.

They listened at the door, then slowly opened it. They were on the first-floor landing – a carpeted balcony running around the central well of the house. The slow tick of a clock drifted up from the ground floor. All other noise was muffled by the thick carpet and the drapes on the walls.

Dust tickled the back of Jack's nose, and to his horror, he felt a sneeze coming on. He pinched his nose furiously until it went away again. A sneeze in this place would echo up and down the hallway until the rafters rang. He tried to breathe only through his mouth.

They crept on to the landing, eyes and ears straining for the slightest sound of alarm. But there was nothing – the house seemed to be empty.

Now that they were inside, Ben took the lead, since he had visited before. He led Jack to the staircase and they made their way cautiously up to the second floor.

Suddenly Ben stopped. Jack looked at him curiously. Ben tapped his nose and mimed taking a deep breath through his nostrils. Jack sniffed and immediately caught a whiff of a strange but powerful animal smell. It was as out of place in this smart townhouse as it was possible to be, and yet it was unmistakeable.

The boys followed their noses to a small door. On the other side there was a narrow staircase leading up into the attics.

They crept up the stairs and found themselves in the servants' quarters. There were no paintings, stuffed animals or deep, rich carpets here. Everything was very basic and functional, and the walls sloped inwards with the roof.

Jack paused to glance out of a tiny window. Down in the street he could see the lamps being lit in the last few minutes of daylight. "We better get a move on," he whispered to Ben.

They were standing in a passage with a threadbare carpet. Plain wooden doors lined the right-hand wall. The boys tiptoed slowly down the corridor, opening the doors and peering inside. They found nothing but bare, empty bedrooms.

At last there was only one door left. It was at the end of the passage and the animal smell was incredibly strong here. Jack glanced at Ben, then turned the handle and carefully pushed the door open.

Beyond was a large, dusty attic. It took up the rest of the top floor of the house and it was dimly lit by three grimy windows. The roof was held up by wooden supports, and old boxes and chests were piled up against the bare plaster of the walls. The animal smell was almost overpowering, but the only living thing in the room was. . .

"Emily!" Ben exclaimed.

Emily was sitting on the floor, tied to a wooden support. At the sound of Ben's voice, she looked up in surprise. She mouthed something Jack couldn't hear and shook her head frantically. Jack put a restraining hand on Ben's shoulder.

Ben mouthed, "What?" and in response Emily looked up at the ceiling.

The boys followed her gaze and immediately realized what had been causing the strong animal odour. The rafters were swathed with bats. Their wings were like black leather; the fur on their bodies was like black, bristly velvet.

Jack guessed that they must be vampires. He remembered Ben saying that there had been about a hundred bats originally. There seemed to be many more than that, now. Sir Donald and his servants had clearly been busy creating more followers.

Ben was looking up at the creatures with undisguised loathing. Jack knew he was seeing more than just vampires. He was seeing the ruination of the Mexican expedition, the tragic deaths of his father and Uncle Edwin, and the destruction of hopes and dreams.

After a moment, Ben crept forward slowly and knelt beside Emily. Her hands were tied behind the wooden post and it took him a few minutes to free them. As soon as her arms were loose she wrapped Ben in an enormous hug. Then she spied something over his shoulder and cried out in alarm.

A vampire bat was dropping down from the ceiling – but even as it fell, it seemed to be swelling and changing. Arms and legs appeared and it landed on feet that hadn't been there a moment before. The form became human –

tall, thin and clad in a black morning suit. It was Mr Brown, the butler.

Jack simply stood and stared in complete astonishment. But Ben was already dragging a stunned Emily towards the door. As they reached it, they turned to face the vampire.

Mr Brown grinned at them through glistening fangs. He stretched out his hands towards them and, instead of fingers, Jack saw that they were still the vicious claws of a vampire bat.

"Come, children," the butler hissed, and lunged at them.

And at that moment, Jack came to himself again. He side-stepped, picked up a wooden chair and smashed it down on the back of Mr Brown's head. The vampire staggered and fell to the floor.

"Run!" Jack shouted.

The butler was already scrambling up from the floorboards, but the friends were through the attic door, and Jack threw it shut in his face before pelting down the stairs after Ben and Emily.

The three of them burst on to the second-floor landing. Stuffed animals flew by in a blur as they raced to the next flight of stairs. The boys could take the stairs two at a time, but Emily in her skirt had to go more slowly, and they couldn't leave her behind.

Mr Brown had reached the landing door, but he didn't seem to be hurrying. "There's no need to run!" he called after them, and his fangs gave him a curious lisp, which was not at all comic. "You cannot escape!"

They were on the first-floor landing now and the butler had reached the top of the stairs above them. "There is nowhere to go," he cried. "Stay and join the Master!"

The friends were at the top of the very last flight of stairs. Jack could see the front door directly ahead. He pounded down the stairs and skidded on the tiles as he reached the hallway. Outside the door, there was still – just a little – sunlight. They would be safe.

Ben reached the door first. His hands closed on the knob and he tugged at it. The door stayed where it was. "It's locked!" he shouted. He yanked again, but it wouldn't budge.

Jack joined Ben at the door and together they tried to haul it open. But it was firmly locked and they were forced to turn back to the hallway, searching frantically for another way out.

Mr Brown was descending the final flight of stairs. He held up the front door key and his smile seemed to split his face in two. "You will belong to the Master," he said and laughed. "Everyone must join him, sooner or later."

"This way!" Emily shouted, and she ran across the hallway to the door that led into the basement, and the tradesman's entrance beyond. It, too, was locked. Ben and Jack threw their combined weight against it, but it was solid oak and would not give.

Mr Brown reached the foot of the stairs, and the three friends backed against the wall.

Jack felt a doorknob pressing into his spine. Out of desperation he grabbed it and turned. The door opened. Jack stumbled through it and just managed to stop himself falling down a narrow flight of stone steps. "In here!" he yelled.

"It's only the cellar—" Emily began, but Ben grabbed her and pushed her in.

The butler's smile vanished and he charged forward. "No!" he bellowed in fury. "You may not defile the holy place!"

The vampire's speed was incredible, quite unlike his previous lazy pace. Ben barely made it through the door after Emily, and he cried out as a claw scraped down his back. But then he was through, and the friends were scrambling to shut the door in Mr Brown's face. There was a lock on this side and, thankfully, a key.

Jack turned the key just as the butler's weight slammed into the door from the other side. This time, the solidity of the oak was in their favour. For the moment, they were safe. But they were locked behind a wooden door with a vampire on the other side, and nowhere to go but deeper into the cellar.

CHAPTER SIXTEEN

The three of them stood at the top of the steps. Ben was craning his neck to look at the scratch down his back.

Emily moved forward to take a look at it for him. The claw had torn Ben's coat and shirt over his right shoulder. In some places it had pierced the skin, and blood was welling up from the cuts. Despite that, it didn't look too severe.

"We'll get a bandage on it when we get out of here," Emily said. "But I think you'll live."

Jack was peering down into the cellar. "What's that light?" he asked.

A golden yellow glow shone up from the room below. Jack crept curiously down the steps into the room, and as he drew closer he realized it was candlelight.

"He said the cellar was out of bounds. . ." Emily murmured as she followed Jack.

"And he called it 'the holy place'," Ben added, almost

walking into his sister as she and Jack stopped at the foot of the stairs.

Just as the attic had smelled of bats, so the cellar smelled of damp. The walls were whitewashed but grimy. The floor was paved with stone slabs. And dusty furniture and boxes were stacked around the edges of the room.

Jack gazed around in awe. It was easy to see because the cellar was lit by hundreds of candles. The two largest were mounted on what looked like some kind of altar at the far end of the room. The altar had apparently been made by tearing up some of the stone slabs from the floor. Dominating it was a huge and terrifying carved effigy of the bat god, Camazotz. The creature towered over the altar, wings spread, fanged mouth snarling. Its eyes radiated hate and Jack looked away with a shiver.

His gaze fell on a pair of smaller golden artefacts that were lying on the altar top. And then his eyes focused on the altar itself. It was stained black with glistening rivers of blood, and next to it was a large, long wooden box.

Suddenly Jack realized that he had been walking towards the altar in fascinated horror. And Ben and Emily weren't far behind.

"Do you think Sir Donald might be in there?" Jack whispered, pointing at the box.

"Probably," Ben whispered back gloomily. "It's the

perfect place for him to sleep – no light can possibly get in to disturb him."

"That blood doesn't look very old," Emily pointed out, looking at the altar.

Jack remembered the story in the paper that Ben had read out. "Hey! You don't think that bloke who washed up in Waterloo – the one with no heart – you don't think 'e was sacrificed here, do you?"

"Yes, I do," Ben snapped. "And I think it's time we were leaving before the same thing happens to us!"

The door at the stop of the stairs was shaking. Mr Brown seemed to have gathered reinforcements. It occurred to Jack that the sun must have set by now, so every vampire in the attic would be awake and ready to assist the butler. The friends could not afford to linger.

"Over there," Ben said quietly, pointing to one corner of the cellar, where the house's supply of coal was piled up and surrounded by a waist-high wall. "There must be a chute to the surface. We can get out that way!"

Getting out sounded like a very good idea to Jack. He followed Ben and Emily over to the coal, instinctively keeping as far from the altar as he could.

Suddenly Emily recoiled in horror. Jack and Ben turned to see what had startled her.

"Oh, dear God," Ben whispered. And then Jack, peering over Ben's shoulder, saw it too.

Two figures lay in the darkest corner of the cellar. Their limbs were caught at strange angles, as if the bodies had just been tossed carelessly aside. It was a man and a woman. They wore the remains of servants' uniforms, but the clothing that covered their top halves had been ripped open and Jack could see that their chests had been literally torn apart. So this is what had become of Sir Donald's former staff. They had been used as human sacrifices to the bat god, Camazotz.

With an effort, Ben turned away. He took hold of Emily and led her away too. "Over here," he said. Next to the pile of coal, a metal chute ran up to a small hatch where the ceiling met the wall.

For Ben and Jack, there was no question of who should go first. Emily protested but they seized her and pushed her up the chute. It was a narrow steel tunnel and its sides were black and filthy. She pulled herself on to it, and immediately slipped back down the smooth, sheer metal. She scrabbled with her feet and kicked the chute. A metallic boom filled the cellar.

The boys pushed her up again, and this time Emily was able to reach the hatch and pull herself the rest of the way. The chute door wasn't locked and it swung open easily when she pushed it. She scrambled out, smeared with coal dust and grime, and turned back to help the boys.

"You next," Jack said to Ben. "You got that cut. You might not be able to push me out on your own, but you can both pull me."

Ben accepted the logic. With Jack pushing and Emily

pulling from above, he was quickly able to clamber up and out. Finally, he and Emily both reached back down for their friend.

Jack took one last look around the cellar. The gold artefacts on the altar spoke to old instincts inside him – pickpocketing instincts born of being poor and cold and hungry. He was filled with a sudden urge to retrieve the valuables. One looked like a small crown, and he recognized the other from the picture he had seen in Adensnap's office – it was the bat statue that Edwin Sherwood had brought back from Mexico. Surely he should at least get that one. . .

The lid of the wooden box next to the altar suddenly started to rise. Jack yelled in shock and took about two seconds to scramble up the chute after his friends.

"We should leave!" he panted as soon as he reached the outside world.

Ben and Emily nodded, and the three of them staggered round the side of the house to the square.

The front door of Sir Donald's house swung open above them. Mr Brown stood there, fangs and claws gone, looking just like a normal, human butler. "Thieves!" he shouted.

A couple further up the street turned to look.

"Stop those children! Stop thief!" bellowed the butler.

Jack, Ben and Emily ran.

CHAPTER SEVENTEEN

Ben and Emily were running west across the square.

"No!" Jack shouted. "This way!" He grabbed Emily and pulled her after him. Ben followed. Now they were running back towards the alleyways between the houses.

"Hyde Park's that way," Jack muttered as their feet pounded on the cobbles. "There's nowhere to hide in a park. This way, we gets closer to home all the time and there's lots of places to go."

Now that the sun had gone down, the alleys ahead of them looked dark and uninviting. Behind them they heard the butler shout, "After them!"

"He's sending the vampires after us!" Emily moaned.

"Then run faster," Ben gasped.

Dry wings fluttered behind them and a strange, high-pitched screeching seemed to echo off the walls. The vampires were chasing in their bat form.

The three ran past the wall of Sir Donald's garden and out into an open-ended mews. This was where the people living in the square stabled their horses. It was lighter here. The sky still glowed with the last faint light of sunset and there were no tall buildings to shade the ground.

Jack glanced back. The luminous sky showed pink down the alley and four fluttering bat shapes were silhouetted against it. Jack looked up and down the mews. If they ran in either direction, they would be caught out in the open.

"Keep going," he said. They ran straight across the mews and into another alley.

Jack didn't know this area of London well. He was aware that Hyde Park lay to the west and Green Park to the south – two wide, empty spaces that he felt they had best avoid. Otherwise, it really wasn't his territory.

Instinct told him that they needed crowds of people and buildings among which to lose their pursuers. He steered Ben and Emily in what he thought was an easterly direction, towards Soho, and prayed that he wasn't wrong.

The friends burst out into the elegant, cobbled thoroughfare of Regent Street. The gaslights were all lit and the Georgian facades of the buildings looked warm and inviting. Hansom cabs trotted up and down its length, but the street was not crowded. It was still too open for Jack's liking.

"We wants a crowd," he muttered. "Crowds is good. Even if the bats turn into humans, they'll find it hard to follow us."

Years of living on the streets had taught Jack that adults could never chase youngsters through a crowd. Children could slip into spaces, and wriggle through gaps that adults could not. And, he reasoned, even if the vampires stayed as bats and searched from the air, what would they see? A mass of heads.

"Down there," Ben gasped, his sides heaving. He wasn't used to running like this. He waved a hand. "Piccadilly. Lots of people. Safe."

Jack glanced south down the street. Sure enough, the bustling chaos of Piccadilly Circus was no more than a minute away. And it was nearly ten o'clock. The theatre-goers would be coming out now. The friends could probably lose themselves in the throng.

Reaching that crowd was another matter, however. Regent Street was very exposed and the vampires were close behind them.

"Right," Jack said. "We goes to Piccadilly, but we takes a more tricky route where it's harder for those bats to get at us. Come on."

"But—" Ben began.

Jack didn't have time to argue, so he grabbed Ben's collar in one hand and Emily's wrist in the other and dragged them both across the street and into a passage.

They were on the outskirts of Soho now, and heading further in. This was the area that London would rather forget. It was bounded by the respectable thoroughfares of Regent Street, Piccadilly and Oxford Street, but within those boundaries lay a dark maze of streets and alleys frequented by London's lowlife.

Jack, Ben and Emily were now in a narrow, winding lane, lined with overhanging buildings that all but blocked out the night sky. The ground was filthy with mud and slime. Nondescript shapes lurked in doorways: the poor of London, already bedding down for the night.

Jack wanted to head well into the labyrinth, then turn south again and approach Piccadilly Circus from a different angle. He plunged onwards. Ben and Emily staggered after him. Behind them came the screeching vampires.

Ahead of them a door opened and firelight flickered out into the evening. A burst of laughter and chatter came with it. It was an inn of some kind, a slum house that made the Admiral Nelson at the docks look respectable.

"We'll go in here," Jack said, and he dragged Emily in before she could protest. Ben followed.

Inside the inn, the air was foul with tobacco and drink and the stink of unwashed people. The place was packed with builders, labourers and market-workers. Someone was playing an out-of-tune piano, but the song could barely be heard over the din of conversations and quarrels. A brown haze hung in the air, fuelled by the smoke from countless pipes and the fire in one corner.

"Oi!" Fingers like steel gripped Jack and Ben's ears in a pinch like a vice. The man hauled them upwards so they had to stand on tiptoe. "I told you street kids before, we don't want your kind in 'ere! This is a respectable 'ouse!"

"Respectable?" Ben gasped, and the man banged their heads together for good measure.

"And I'll 'ave none of your lip. You gets out of 'ere, right now. And you, girly. Out!"

Ben and Jack were dragged through the crowd and thrown back out into the street. Emily wasn't far behind. The door slammed in their faces and Jack immediately scanned the sky for bats.

Ben vainly tried to dust himself down. "Just our luck," he said. "The one public house in Soho with a sense of pride!"

"Come on," Jack replied wearily. He couldn't see the bats – perhaps they had lost them, for the time being.

He led his friends on through the winding alleys, hoping that his sense of direction was still working. Every now and then there was an oil lamp or a burning torch to light their way, but the pools of darkness in between were deep.

Emily gasped as a man-sized figure loomed up at them.

"Bloomin' kids," the man muttered, and went on his way into the night. Emily sighed with relief.

Ahead was the glimmer of gaslight, and the noise of a crowd. Jack had never heard a more cheerful sound. It was men and women and children, real people out for an evening in town and not the disciples of a demon god. A minute later Jack stumbled out on to the main street. He'd done it. They had circled round in the maze of Soho, and reached Piccadilly Circus after all.

"Keep going," Jack muttered, and they ducked into the crowd. Jack glanced back. "I think we're clear," he said.

"No," Ben disagreed. He jerked his head up. Jack followed his gaze and saw a cluster of bats above them. It split into two, and the bats flew off into the side alleys.

Jack lowered his gaze to the entrances, feeling sick with despair. Perhaps he had been *wrong* about crowds. They were a menace. Men and women were coming and going all the time. Some of the people now entering Piccadilly Circus were probably vampires, but once they had assumed their human forms, how could he recognize them?

Someone bumped into him from behind and he cried out in alarm. A bearded man looked at him strangely.

"Sorry, mate," Jack said, feeling foolish.

Emily and Ben were rapidly reaching the same conclusion.

"They could be anywhere," Emily said. "Anywhere and *anyone* at all!"

Ben looked from left to right to left again, searching for a way out. He had never felt so trapped. Then he noticed a carriage working its way through the throng – not a hansom cab but a real carriage – its passengers enclosed in their own little cabin. His eyes fell on the couple inside – a smart, middle-aged pair – and an idea occurred to him. "Come with me," he said to Jack and Emily.

They wormed their way to the carriage as quickly as they could and Ben pulled the door open. He bundled Emily and Jack inside, then climbed up after them and pulled the door shut before the couple in the carriage could protest.

The couple stared at them with open mouths. The man's face was turning red. "What the blazes do you think you're doing?" he demanded. "Driver! Driver, I say. . ."

"I hope you don't mind, sir," Ben said in his most polite voice. "It's a dare, you see. We need to get across town without being seen."

A slow smile spread over the man's face. "A dare, eh?"

"Well, really," declared the woman, "this is all very well but—"

"So, ma'am," interrupted Emily, as sweetly as she possibly could. "If we could share your carriage for a while – and we'll pay, of course. . ."

"Now, Cecilia," put in the man, "perhaps we can accommodate these young people. Boys will be boys – although I'm not sure I approve of dragging young girls into this, y'know." His eyes narrowed. "Who's the dare with?"

"Oh," Ben said casually, "a bunch of Etonian roughs. . ."

"Etonians!" The man exclaimed and thumped his cane against the roof. "Driver! Make haste! Double your speed!" He chuckled and looked back at the friends. "Always good to give 'em one in the eye. Where y'going to?"

Their new friends dropped them off almost at the gates to Bedford Square. When they got out of the carriage, there was no sign of bats or pursuers of any kind.

"What was that about Etonians?" Jack asked as they walked the last few steps to Ben and Emily's front door. "What are they?"

"They're boys who go to Eton School," Ben explained. "I saw the man's tie, you see, and I could tell that he went to Winchester School, like my father. There's always been great competition between the two schools, so I guessed he wouldn't be able to resist the chance to get one over Eton."

"Oh, I see," Jack said. Like so many other things, it was a glimpse into a world Jack had never known about before. He let it pass.

Soon they stood, side by side, looking up at the Coles' house.

"I'm not looking forward to this," Ben muttered as they climbed the steps and he opened the door.

Mrs Mills pounced. She was not a tall woman but she

was an impressive sight, nonetheless, as she bore down upon them, clad in respectable black. "Master Benedict! Miss Emily! Where have you been?" she exclaimed. "Do you know what time it is? And look at the state of you! What *have* you been doing? You can forget about dinner. You will go straight to your rooms and –" She saw Jack for the first time. He was lurking at the back. "And who is this?" Her eyes narrowed.

Emily tried to say something. "We—"

Mrs Mills immediately put a finger to her lips. "No, Miss Emily, not tonight. And as for you, Master Benedict, you have obviously been up to no good at all. . ."

"How right you are, Mrs Mills," remarked a man's voice.

As one they all wheeled round to face the newcomer, and Mrs Mills gave a small gasp of surprise.

"What an unexpected pleasure," she declared. "What can we do for you, Sir Donald?"

CHAPTER EIGHTEEN

Looking smart and respectable, in a black coat and top hat, Sir Donald climbed the steps towards them with a red gleam in his eyes.

Ben realized too late that they shouldn't have come home. Mr Brown had surely recognized him and, of course, Sir Donald knew exactly where Ben and Emily lived. Then Ben remembered that Sir Donald needed an invitation to enter a private home. Quickly, he ushered Jack and Emily into the house, past Mrs Mills who stood in the doorway. Once he had made sure that everyone was inside, Ben turned back to face the vampire god.

"How pleasant to see you back, sir!" Mrs Mills was saying, rather flustered. "I had no idea the expedition had returned. Is Mr Cole with you? Of course, I can—"

"Thank you, Mrs Mills, thank you." Sir Donald had reached the top step. "I wish it were as pleasant for me to be here. Sadly, I have to report that Master Benedict has behaved very badly today."

Mrs Mills frowned at Ben. "How so, Sir Donald?" she asked.

"I have good reason to believe that these three young people broke into my house this afternoon," Sir Donald explained.

Mrs Mills looked horrified. "Master Benedict! How could you?" she demanded.

"I. . ." Ben began.

Sir Donald smiled. "Now, Mrs Mills, I'm sure it was nothing but youthful high spirits. And if I might just come in for a moment, madam, I'm certain we can settle this amicably."

"Well, Sir Donald—" Mrs Mills replied slowly.

"No!" Ben exclaimed, stepping forward and glaring up at Sir Donald, who was standing just outside the door. "You may not come in!"

"Really, Master Benedict!" Mrs Mills said in exasperation. "Sir Donald, you can—"

"*You may not come in!*" Ben insisted. "I'm sorry, Mrs Mills, I didn't want to have to say this –" he glared at Sir Donald again – "but this man and my father had a . . . disagreement in Mexico. He's the reason I came back early. They became enemies. My father was quite clear, Mrs Mills. Sir Donald will never again be welcome in our house."

Sir Donald put on a baffled smile and shrugged at Mrs Mills. "What can I say, madam? I have no idea what the young man is talking about. Perhaps some tropical fever has touched his mind. . ."

"Well. . ." For the first time, the housekeeper looked uncertain. "It *is* Sir Donald, Master Benedict. He's always been your father's friend."

"He is not my father's friend any more," Ben stated firmly.

A dark, heavy growl filled the air. It seemed to come from a throat much larger than Sir Donald's, but when he spoke again, it was in Sir Donald's usual voice. "Friendship or not, Master Cole, you have my property."

"I don't have anything of yours," Ben snapped. And with an air of authority that Jack and Emily had never seen in him before, he walked right up to the door and faced the vampire god. "Now." His voice was almost a hiss. "Listen to me. The master of this house says that you may not enter! *Go!*"

Sir Donald's eyes had narrowed to red slits. "Your father and Sherwood thought they could fight me, and they failed. Do you really think you can fare better?"

Ben smiled, took a step back, and shut the door in his face. After a moment they heard footsteps receding.

Mrs Mills, Emily and Jack just stood and stared. Ben's smile was triumphant and he looked stronger and more confident than Jack had ever seen him.

"Mrs Mills, we'll have our dinner now," Ben said. "Kindly have Evans set the table for three." He put an arm around Jack's shoulders. "This is our friend Jack. He'll be staying with us for a few days, so while we eat,

169

have Tillet make up the spare bed for him, please."

Jack swallowed and blinked furiously. For the first time in years he felt his eyes fill with tears and he was determined not to show it.

"And I hurt my shoulder today," Ben added, "so I'd like you to look at it."

Mrs Mill's mouth moved once or twice, like a fish's. There was something about the new Ben that she could not argue with. "Very well, Master Benedict," she said. "Dinner will be served in half an hour. If you wish to get ready in your rooms, I'll bring you up some warm water."

Jack and Ben were sitting in Ben's room while Mrs Mills saw to Ben's injury. Ben drew in his breath sharply as she cleaned the cut.

"It's a nasty scratch," she said. "You should be more careful. Whatever did this ruined a good coat." She finished dressing the wound and stood up. "That should set you straight. Try not to move your arm too much for the next few days."

Mrs Mills crossed to the wardrobe and withdrew two pairs of trousers. She eyed them carefully, then shook her head and put one back. She gave the pair she was holding to Ben and pulled out another pair for Jack. "You look a little longer in the leg than Master Benedict," she told him. "These will do you better. Master Benedict can show you where the clean shirts are. Now, I'll leave you both to change."

As she passed, Jack could have sworn she gave him a very faint smile and a wink. He suddenly realized that Mrs Mills was quite looking forward to having another boy to look after.

She paused at the door. "Your father trusted you to me, Master Benedict. I will require an explanation, in due course," she said.

"You will have one," Ben replied amiably. "In due course."

The friends couldn't talk while the maids were serving dinner. Emily waited impatiently for them to finish ladling out the soup and leave the room. Then she smiled and looked at Ben. "Sir Donald thought you were lying," she said cheerfully. "You didn't know he was right, did you?"

Ben frowned. "What do you mean?"

Emily laughed, and held up the journal triumphantly.

Her brother snatched it from her in delight. "Father's diary!" he exclaimed.

"I wanted to tell you," Emily said. "But I never had the chance. The butler caught me, but not before I'd found the journal and hidden it in my apron. And look –" She reached over and opened the book up so they could all see it. The pages were covered in a grid full of symbols and letters. "It's the translation table that Father worked out," Emily explained. "If we can get that incantation from Professor Adensnap then I think we can use this to translate it!"

"Oh, Em!" cried Ben happily. "This is great news. It means there's still a chance we can defeat Sir Donald!"

"What does the rest of the diary say?" Jack asked.

"I'll look at it while we eat," Emily replied.

"And what was all that stuff about the 'master of the house'?" Jack questioned Ben.

Ben shrugged. "Mrs Mills didn't realize what I meant, but Sir Donald did. Now that Father's dead, *I'm* the master. And father told me Sir Donald and his vampires can't enter a house if they're not invited."

"Well, that's another piece of good news," Jack said. "At least we know that we are safe from vampires while we're in this house."

Ben nodded and turned to Emily, who was clearly immersed in the contents of the notebook, which she had propped up against the water jug. "What does the diary say?" he asked.

"Apparently there were two levels of meaning in the hieroglyphs at the cave," Emily began. "The top one was like a summary, and that's what Father translated. He was still working on the rest. . ."

"Yes, but what does his translation *say*?" Ben demanded impatiently.

Emily frowned at the pages. "It's all rather grand. 'Woe to ye, doleful travellers that come to this place. . .' We already know much of it. Yes, Camazotz was banished, as the professor said. The priests of Chac put him to sleep for a millennium in that cave, by using the professor's ritual, I presume. There's a description of who Camazotz is and what he does. He and his minions can change form from bat to human and back again. . ."

"In Mexico, he just killed people," Ben said. "But he can create new vampires as well. Does it say how he does that?"

Emily flicked through the notes. "Mostly he just drinks blood," she agreed. "So do all his servants. They can even live off animals if they must. But they can also turn humans into vampires like themselves."

"Yes, but how?" Ben asked sharply. "*How?*"

Emily looked surprised at his vehemence. "Well, if a human is bitten by a vampire three times –" she peered more closely at the page – "then that person becomes a vampire themselves. If a person is bitten fewer than three times, then they just fall sick and usually die."

Ben breathed a sigh of relief. "Thank goodness for that," he said.

Emily's hand flew to her mouth. "You were thinking of Father! You thought he might be a vampire! Oh, Ben, that's horrible!" she cried.

"But he isn't," Ben said. "He was only bitten once. So he's resting in peace."

"And tomorrow," Jack put in, "we can take the translation to the professor and see if we can't lay Camazotz to rest for another millennium!"

CHAPTER NINETEEN

Jack woke suddenly. He lay still for a moment as his brain caught up with where he was. His dreams had been full of bats and dust and fiery eyes, but some part of him had known he was safe as long as he was in a house. It felt strange to Jack to be lying in a proper bed. He was in the Coles' spare room, and the bed was soft and warm and comfortable, but he was surrounded by unfamiliar objects and clean smells that he had never known before.

His eyes settled on the grey shape of the chair next to his bed, and the darker patch of grey that was the pile of clothes laid out for him by Mrs Mills. And while his eyes adjusted to the dark, his ears were straining for whatever had woken him up. Instincts honed by twelve years of living on the streets of London told him that something was wrong.

Then he heard it again. It was the faintest thud of a cautious footstep on the stair. But it was past midnight and Jack knew everyone was already upstairs. So who was this newcomer?

He slid out of bed and crossed the room silently. The long, white nightshirt brushed strangely against his legs. He reached the door and opened it gently, just a crack.

His room was at the top of the first flight of stairs. White moonlight shone up the stairwell from the hall below, and halfway up the stairs was the dark shape of a man. Jack's heart pounded for a moment, but then he remembered and grinned – as far as he knew, no one had yet invited a vampire into the house. Whoever was coming up the stairs could only be human. He let the figure come closer. . .

Just as the man was about to reach the top, Jack stepped out in front of him. The landing behind him was dark and he knew he must appear as a pale and ghostly figure in his nightshirt. He raised his arms above his head. *"Wooo-oo-oo!"*

The man screamed, stepped back and missed a stair. He plummeted back down the staircase and crashed into the gong at the bottom. Its boom echoed around the house. Jack ran nimbly downstairs after him and leaped on top of the intruder. The breath rushed out of the man's lungs and he collapsed. Jack pressed him face down into the carpet and knelt astride him. He grabbed the man's arm and twisted it behind his back, up to the shoulder blade.

"Just wait nice and quiet," he said.

A light appeared at the top of the stairs. Ben came

slowly down towards Jack, a lamp in one hand and a poker in the other. Emily followed.

"Uninvited guest," said Jack cheerfully.

They crowded round him and stared. The man lay helplessly on the floor peering up at them. There was nothing special about him. He had a stubbly face and thinning hair. His clothes were dark and he reeked of tobacco.

"He pulled you out of some doss house, didn't he?" Jack demanded. "He must be desperate."

The man's eyes darted from one unfriendly face to another. "Who yer talking about?" he asked.

"Sir Donald," Ben said quietly.

"I dunno who—"

"Solid-looking bloke," interrupted Jack. "With a top hat and a moustache."

The man didn't say anything but they all saw the glimmer of recognition in his eyes.

"Who's there? Master Benedict, is that you?" Another light glimmered upstairs, and Mrs Mills came slowly down out of the shadows. Behind her they could just see the shapes of Tillet and Evans. Mrs Mills gasped when she saw the little group.

"We caught a prowler, Mrs Mills," Ben told her. "Nothing important."

Mrs Mills was aghast. "Nothing important? It's outrageous! This is a respectable household! We'll send for the police at once. . ."

"No," said Ben immediately. "No one goes outside."

"But, Master Benedict. . ."

Jack and Emily glanced at each other. Any of them would be in danger if they left the house. Outside, they were fair game for Sir Donald – and that included the prowler himself. They could guess how Sir Donald would reward failure, and not even a burglar deserved that.

But Mrs Mills didn't know about the danger, and sending for the police would be the natural thing to do in the circumstances. Emily realized they needed to convince Mrs Mills to wait until daylight. She thought quickly. "He might have friends outside, Mrs Mills," she pointed out. "There might be more men lurking out there, ready to waylay us. No, I think Ben's right. We should wait until morning."

"But I don't—" the burglar began, and Jack casually trod on his face. "*Mmph!*"

Mrs Mills pursed her lips, but they could see Emily's logic sinking in.

"Jack, you and I will tie this man up in the kitchen," Ben said. "You! How did you get in?" he quizzed the intruder.

"*Mmph*," said the burglar again, until Jack removed his foot from the man's mouth. "Pantry window," the prowler muttered sullenly.

"Then we'll lock the pantry door, and every other downstairs room with an outside window too. In the morning we'll summon the police," Ben announced.

Once they had secured the burglar and the house, Jack drew Ben aside. "Sir Donald is resorting to desperate measures," he said. "He must be afraid of us. Which means we need to be extra careful."

"Don't worry, Jack. There's nowhere else for a burglar to get in," Ben said reassuringly. "And we won't open the door to anyone. We'll be safe for tonight."

"And tomorrow?" asked Jack.

"I expect the sun will come up. It usually does," Ben told him cheerfully, heading upstairs to bed. "Now get some sleep and stop worrying. We'll soon get rid of Sir Donald."

But Jack had an uneasy feeling that the trouble was only just beginning.

CHAPTER TWENTY

"Marvellous!" declared Professor Adensnap. He slowly turned the diary over and over in his hands as if he could scarcely believe it was real. "This is like gold dust! No! More valuable even than that!"

The morning had dawned bright and sunny, the police had been summoned and, with some relief, Ben had delivered the prowler into their custody. As soon as that had been accomplished, the friends had hurried to the museum to see Professor Adensnap.

It was now eleven o'clock and Jack, Ben and Emily were once again squeezed on to the settee in the professor's office, while Adensnap himself was studying Harrison Cole's journal with undisguised delight.

"Does this mean you believe our story, Professor?" inquired Emily, remembering his doubts of yesterday.

Adensnap peered at her over his glasses. "My dear, let's just say that I believe you have appeared in my office with a priceless linguistic tool today which you did not have yesterday. I have no reason to doubt your account of how you came by it. But part of me still hopes that this is all an elaborate hoax."

"Will it help, Professor?" Ben asked impatiently. "Will you be able to translate the ritual now?"

"Patience, Master Cole, patience. Let us see, shall we?" The professor took out the parchment from the Spanish missionary that contained the banishment ritual. He laid it flat on his desk, then opened up the diary and put the two side by side. His fingers traced the hieroglyphics of the ritual, then the translation table that Harrison Cole had so carefully constructed. His lips moved silently.

The friends held their breath.

"Hmm," Adensnap murmured.

Then: "Aha. . ."

Then: "Hmm," again.

"Please, Professor!" Emily burst out.

Adensnap looked up and sighed. "The short answer is, yes, I think I will be able to translate it," he said. "But slowly. Your father never expected these notes to be used by anyone but him. Doubtless he intended to write his work up so that others could follow it, upon his return to England. But at present these notes are in no logical order, his notation is highly idiosyncratic and his handwriting, it must be said, is not of the best. It will be slow going, I warn you."

"Perhaps I can help, sir?" suggested Emily. "I know

my father's writing, and I've been doing some studying on my own. Let me show you."

She joined the professor at his desk and leaned over the parchment. "Look, the writing comes in two forms. Some of it just seems to be symbols that represent whole words, but the rest is words built out of syllables. It's not always obvious which is which."

Adensnap's eyes widened behind his glasses. "Bless me! An educated young girl! And I do see it's not so straightforward as A-B-C." He pointed at a short passage of hieroglyphs. "I imagine this symbol on its own might have several meanings and the symbol after it helps describe which one."

"That's exactly what I thought, Professor," Emily agreed enthusiastically. "Furthermore. . ."

The boys, abandoned and forgotten on the settee, stared at this unexpected meeting of minds.

"You getting on, then?" Jack asked conversationally.

". . .the syllables seem to be written down with a kind of harmonic theme, so that the vowel of the last syllable matches the vowel of the syllable that comes immediately before it. . ." Emily explained.

"We'll just sit here, shall we?" Ben put in.

". . .But words that have differing vowels in the last two syllables might actually end at the last consonant. . ." pointed out the professor.

"I mean, don't mind us. . ." Jack said.

". . .indeed, so there need to be indicators that the

final vowel is to be voiced, like this," Emily continued.

"Come on, Jack." Ben gave his friend a nudge. "Let me show you round the museum."

"Sunset!" Adensnap cried a couple of hours later, as Ben and Jack opened the door to his office. "That's what it means!"

The boys glanced at each other, then sidled into the room. Ben had taken Jack to see the Elgin Marbles, the friezes that had once adorned the front of the Parthenon in Athens. Jack had been relieved to learn that there were ancient civilizations that *hadn't* sacrificed people to demon gods. But neither boy's mind was really on the cultural treasures. Both of them were thinking of their struggle to defeat Sir Donald and hoping that Emily and the professor would be able to translate the ancient banishment ritual, which might prove the key to their success.

"See," said the professor. He pointed at a hieroglyph. "We know this is sun*rise*, so this must be sun*set*."

"So," Emily responded, "the whole thing reads, 'Gather the rose *at sunset* and crush the leaves. . .'"

"Exactly, my dear! Oh, hello." Adensnap had glanced up at last and noticed the boys waiting. "Good news, lads. I think we have it."

"Roses at sunset?" asked Ben.

"Ah. Yes," Adensnap confirmed. "You see, the

banishment ritual appears to consist of an incantation and a potion."

"We need to have both," Emily explained. "We have the words of the incantation on this parchment, but we have to prepare a potion as well."

"What kind of potion?" Ben inquired.

"One with roses, I 'spect," Jack put in.

"Not just any kind of rose, though," Ben said slowly. "You mean the blood rose, don't you? That's why it's on the parchment."

"Exactly," agreed Adensnap. "*Rosa sanguina*, or *la rosa de la sangre*, as our Jesuit friend calls it. He says here that it's 'a shrub whose bite is a most violent poison to his servants who walk by night, and whose essence, distilled in a potion, is a bane to He Who Walks by Darkness'."

The boys looked blankly at him.

"Its thorns are poisonous to vampires," said Emily impatiently, "and if it's made into a potion, it can banish Camazotz!"

"But only when used with the appropriate incantation," added the professor.

Ben sank slowly on to the professor's settee.

"The potion has to be prepared in a very specific way," Emily continued, reading from her notes. "Leaves of the rose have to be plucked at sunset, and added to the potion at sunrise. Then Camazotz must be cornered in what it calls 'a place of power'. The potion must be sprinkled on him at the same time as these words here are read out. . ."

She ran her finger along the unfamiliar syllables.

"*U bah ti akot hasaw-chan,*
Camazotz u hun katun.
Camazotz kin winal tun,
Chuwen keh tu bah ha atun."

Jack craned his neck to study the writing. "This'll be where it talks about the rose, then?" he said, pointing at one of the hieroglyphs, which looked just like a flower.

"That's it," said Emily.

Jack ran his eyes over the rest of the parchment. "And what's this?" he asked. Every time the rose hieroglyph appeared, it was preceded by what looked like a mass of squiggly lines that reminded Jack of a bonfire.

"We assume it's some kind of qualifier," Emily told him. "So it's telling us something more about the rose. But we don't know exactly what."

Jack looked hopefully at Ben to see if he had any bright ideas, but Ben was looking despondent. "What's wrong?" Jack asked his friend.

"The blood rose is a Mexican flower," Ben said quietly. "We are in England."

"Oh," said Jack. For a moment it seemed like a crushing blow to their hopes. He rallied determinedly. "We'll go to Covent Garden market. All kinds of flowers there. Bound to be some. . ."

"I very much doubt it, Jack," Ben told him.

Adensnap spoke, and there was suddenly steel in the professor's mild tones – one of the occasional reminders that he was not just an absent-minded old man. "Have faith in your elders and betters, Master Cole," he said. "I showed the parchment to a colleague in the botany department, and happily he knows just where we can find some blood roses!"

He opened a drawer and delved inside it, while Ben held his breath. "I have it here somewhere . . . couple of years ago now. . . Bless me, when will I learn to file properly? Aha!" He straightened up and tossed a pamphlet on to the desk. "I think you'll find this much closer than the Yucatan."

Ben picked up the pamphlet and his face lit up. " 'Announcing the opening to the general public of the Palm House at the Royal Botanical Gardens, Kew'," he read. " 'An engineering marvel of our age: a warm, moist climate all the year round for the growing of tropical trees, shrubs and bushes.' "

"M'colleague says a botanist he knows has special permission to keep some blood roses there," Adensnap explained. "Chap collects roses, but this variety doesn't really take to our climate."

He took the pamphlet back and stuffed it into a pocket. "This evening, at sunset, we must be at Kew."

The day passed with aching slowness. The ancient parchment specified that the rose had to be plucked at sunset, so sunset it would have to be. It was the last day of May. The professor's almanac said sunset would be at 9.06 p.m.

Ben wrote a note to Mrs Mills, assuring her that all was well and that they would be home as soon as possible. Then he gave a boy a penny and asked him to deliver the letter to the house in Bedford Square.

Eventually, Professor Adensnap decided it was time for them to set off. But before they left his office, he turned to Ben and peered gravely at his young friend. "Master Cole," he said grimly. "You have done nothing but outwit Camazotz. You escaped from him in Mexico. So far in England, you have broken into his house, eluded his vampires, and shut a door in his face."

Ben felt very pleased with himself. But the professor's next words soon changed that.

"The Camazotz of legend would not forgive any of those insults," Adensnap warned. He tapped Ben lightly on the chest with his umbrella. "I'm afraid you are now this demon's greatest enemy. Be mindful of that fact. And be careful!"

It was a sobering note on which to start their journey.

CHAPTER TWENTY-ONE

The friends waited outside the museum while the professor hailed a four-wheeler to ferry them to Kew. A cab-driver caught the professor's eye, and steered his carriage over to the kerb for them.

As it drew up, Jack got a strange feeling that someone was watching him. He quickly glanced around, but all he could see were the usual crowds of people about their everyday business: walking along the pavement, buying newspapers, waving down cabs. He told himself that he was worrying about nothing – with so many people about, somebody's gaze was bound to fall on him – but he couldn't shake his sense of unease.

He transferred his attention to the far side of the road, but just then the cab stopped in front of him, blocking his view. For a split second he thought he'd seen a tall, dark figure looking in his direction, but he couldn't be sure he hadn't just imagined it. He comforted himself that there was still plenty of daylight, so no vampires should be about, and smiled at the thought that perhaps some street urchin had been sizing him up, in his smart new clothes – much as Jack himself had sized up others in the past.

"After you," the professor said cheerfully, and Ben, Jack and Emily piled in.

The driver seemed delighted to undertake such a long journey – Kew was more than ten miles away. He flicked his whip over the horses and the cab set off.

They didn't talk much about their mission – they were conscious of the driver well within earshot. Lulled by the rhythm of the cab, Jack watched the outskirts of London rattle by and marvelled. It was the furthest he had ever travelled in his life. Ben had sailed across the Atlantic and back: this was Jack's equivalent.

The cab trundled down Piccadilly towards Kensington. The buildings began to thin away and Jack had the feeling that London was losing its grip on them as the hustle and bustle of the great city was slowly but steadily left behind.

By the time they reached Hammersmith they were well and truly out in the countryside. Jack looked about him in amazement. He had never imagined such huge, green spaces were possible. The farms and fields of Middlesex stretched away in either direction, and for the first time in his life Jack realized he was breathing air that didn't smell of coal.

The roads were just packed dirt, no longer paved, and

the four-wheeler bounced in the ruts left by a hundred other carts and carriages. Just after Chiswick they took a left turning towards Kew and clattered over the wooden, seven-arched bridge across the Thames – this far upstream, the river actually looked clear and inviting. Finally the carriage drew up in front of the carved stone pillars which marked the main gate of the Royal Botanical Gardens.

The gate was shut.

An attendant eventually appeared – in response to the professor banging his umbrella on the ornate filigree of the black iron gates – and explained that it was not just the gate but the whole gardens that were. . .

"Closed! What do you mean, closed?" Adensnap thundered.

The man wore a dark coat and cap as a kind of uniform. It gave him some kind of authority with the public but none at all with the professor. "It's almost sunset, sir. . ." the attendant explained.

"Exactly! Look." Adensnap pulled out a card and handed it to the man. "Adensnap, British Museum. Very important research. I need to do it now, and it's vital we're not disturbed!"

The man read the card. "Curator of South American Artefacts?" he queried.

"Confound it, don't be impudent," Adensnap said impatiently. "Well, are you going to let us in?"

The attendant ran a despairing eye over the small

group and relented. "Well, I could let you in for a moment, sir," he said with a sigh.

"A moment's all we need!" Adensnap assured him. "Lead on!"

Jack noticed the Palm House from some way off. It was built on a small rise, overlooking the gardens and a lake which reflected the building like a mirror. The building itself was unlike any Jack had ever seen before. It was an enormous glasshouse, supported by a delicate, white metal framework. It gleamed in the evening sunshine and Jack thought it looked as though someone had created a cathedral out of spun sugar.

"Now," said Adensnap to the attendant as they reached the door of the Palm House, "we're looking for the blood rose. D'you know where that is?"

"Blood rose, sir?" The man scratched his head. "I just help look after the grounds. You'd have to ask someone as knows—"

"Never mind," Adensnap interrupted brusquely. "Just leave us here, m'good man. We'll find it, never fear."

The attendant looked unhappy at the thought of letting them roam alone, but his awe of a professor was apparently strong enough to overcome his objections. "Right you are, sir," he said. He pulled out a keyring and thumbed through the jingling mass of keys for the right one. He unlocked the door and pulled it open. "I'll be waiting for you at the gate, sir, when you've finished," he added politely, before making his way back across the gardens.

One by one the friends entered the Palm House and the warm, moist air of the tropics enveloped them.

"Whew!" Jack said. He waved a hand in front of his face but it had no effect. "Was Mexico like this?"

"Hotter," Ben replied quietly. "It felt as if the air in your lungs was being sucked out. We were sweating from every pore, but the air was already so humid, the sweat couldn't evaporate. So we felt as if we were trapped inside a giant steam bath." A grim look passed across Ben's face as he remembered his experiences in the Mexican jungle.

Emily put a hand on her brother's arm. "At least Sir Donald isn't here, though, Ben," she reminded him.

Ben seemed to come to himself. "No, he isn't," he agreed. "And you do get used to the heat."

Not only was the Palm House the size of a cathedral, but the inside was laid out rather like a church. The building was shaped like a tall cross, with two short arms halfway down. Two long, central aisles ran from one end of the building to the other. The spaces between the aisles were packed with wooden tubs like vast, waist-high gardening boxes. It was in these that the trees and shrubs were planted. The floor was an iron grating and water trickled unseen beneath their feet. The house was well lit by the light of the setting sun as it streamed through the glass walls. But Jack realized that they would find themselves in darkness as soon as the sun had fully set.

They walked forward to the middle of the building and looked up and down one of the central aisles.

"Well, there's four of us," Adensnap said. "Two of us can take this end of the house, two of us the other end, and between us we should find—"

Ben shook his head. "No need, sir," he remarked quietly. He closed his eyes and inhaled deeply, smelling the air. He turned this way and that, finally settling on an aisle to their left. He drew a final breath. "It's this way."

"That's very impressive, Ben," Emily said.

He shook his head again. "Once you've smelt the scent of this rose, you'll never forget it," he told her.

And there in front of them was the blood rose itself, a small bush nestling in a tub at the far end of the Palm House. They clustered around to look at the dark green shiny leaves, and the blood-red roses. The plant looked less impressive than it had in Mexico. Even in the humid Palm House, perhaps, the climate did not quite agree with it.

The cruel, curved thorns and the heady scent of the roses set it apart.

Jack incautiously put his nose to the petals, sniffed and promptly recoiled, gagging. "I see what you mean about the smell," he told Ben, who smiled.

"A bit smaller than the last time you saw it, eh what?" remarked the professor.

"We only need a little, sir," Emily pointed out.

"Very true, very true," Adensnap agreed. He pulled his

watch out of his waistcoat pocket and checked the time. Then he glanced up at the sun. "Almost sunset," he said and turned to Emily. "Will you do the honours, m'dear? Pick a whole stem. We can put it in some water."

Emily reached down and carefully wrapped her fingers around the base of the nearest stem, taking care to avoid the thorns. She kept her eyes on the sun through the window. The skyline around Kew was dark and jagged with the silhouettes of trees, and Emily watched as the glowing golden orb gradually melted into the black treeline. As the sun vanished, she plucked the stem and held it up for all to see. "We have it," she declared and put it into her bag.

The boys grinned; Adensnap politely applauded. "Now we have a potion to brew," he said.

"Professor!" The call rang around the Palm House and they all turned to look.

Jack recognized the voice, though he couldn't see the speaker. It was the attendant.

"Just coming," Adensnap replied cheerfully. "We've got what we came for."

"It's just that your colleague's arrived, sir."

The friends looked at each other quizzically.

"I wasn't expecting anyone," Adensnap murmured.

They started walking back, through the gloomy twilight that now engulfed the Palm House, towards the entrance. As they turned the corner to face the door, they saw two figures standing in front of it – the attendant, and a tall man wearing a long cloak and a wide-brimmed hat.

The attendant's face lit up. "Ah, there you are, Professor! I was just saying to your colleague here. . ."

Even as the attendant spoke, the other man let his long dark cloak slip to the floor and removed his hat. "Sunset," he hissed. "At last I can move freely!" His eyes fell on Ben and shone with a horribly familiar red gleam.

Ben stopped dead in his tracks. It was the butler, Mr Brown.

CHAPTER TWENTY-TWO

"Get behind me, Em," Ben said sharply, moving quickly to stand in front of his sister.

Jack remembered the tall dark figure he thought he'd seen outside the museum, and his uneasy feeling that someone was watching him. Clearly Mr Brown had been following the friends – well wrapped up against the sun in cloak and hat. "What did you do? Help yourself to a lift on the back of our four-wheeler?" Jack demanded.

"It seemed the easiest way to keep track of you," Mr Brown confirmed. He smiled, and his grin continued to grow until it was splitting his face from ear to ear. It was hideous to look at and yet oddly mesmerizing.

"Good Lord!" exclaimed Adensnap, aghast. And Jack realized that this was the first time the professor had been confronted by a real vampire.

The attendant was staring, too. "What—" he began.

Mr Brown casually reached out with both hands, grabbed the man's head and twisted. There was a sickening snapping sound and the attendant dropped lifeless to the iron grating. Mr Brown stooped to retrieve the attendant's keys and then turned back to lock the Palm House door. He seemed to be in no hurry.

He was dropping the keys in his pocket when Emily ran at him and slashed at his face with the thorny blood rose. The butler's eyes widened in surprise, but he ducked aside just in time and the thorns missed him by a fraction of an inch. He lashed out with one hand and caught Emily across the jaw, flinging her into a palm tree. She cracked her head on the corner of a tub and crumpled to the floor unconscious.

"Em!" Ben cried in alarm.

Seeing Ben distracted, Mr Brown turned to attack him. But Jack had been in many fights, and he had read the butler's body language. As the vampire flew towards Ben, Jack shoved his friend firmly out of the way.

Mr Brown landed on the iron grating where Ben had been standing just a split second before. Immediately, he wheeled back round to face the boys, hissing with annoyance. He raised his hands, and the fingers started to shift and transform into vicious talons.

As the vampire prepared for his next attack, Jack saw Adensnap run forward and drag Emily's unconscious form out of harm's way. He could see no sign of the blood rose and reasoned that she must have dropped it as she fell. Pushing Ben ahead of him, Jack edged around

Mr Brown until he and Ben had their backs to the spot where Emily had fallen.

The vampire turned to keep the boys in front of him and then slowly advanced on them. Instinctively they backed away, Jack constantly feeling behind him for the tub that Emily had fallen against.

"Benedict Cole," the vampire snarled. "The Master commands that you shall die – slowly – in pain and terror. The exact details he left to me." He looked hungrily at Jack and licked his lips. "Young, healthy, full of life and vigour – you will make a rich feast and I will savour every drop. I will drink and drink until you are empty."

Jack felt the plant tub behind him and immediately reached inside, his fingers searching for the blood rose.

Ben realized what his friend was doing and attempted to buy him some time. "What about my sister, Emily?" he shouted. "And the professor? What will you do with them?"

"I will change the old man," Mr Brown said thoughtfully. "His blood will be worn and tired, but there is knowledge in that head that might be of use to the Master. And the girl, another of the Master's enemies," he mused and then chuckled. "Yes. I have it. The girl I shall change too, and she, Cole, will feast upon you. Your last sight will be of your sister taking her first meal as a vampire. The justice will please the Master." Mr Brown smiled again as if he had reached a clever conclusion. "And now, Cole boy, it is time for you to watch your friend die." And with that, the vampire launched himself at Jack.

Jack's search for the blood rose had been utterly unsuccessful, but just as he saw the butler lunging towards him, he felt a sharp pain in the palm of his right hand, and knew that he must have found the rose's thorny stem. Heedless of the pain, he grasped it firmly and brought it round between himself and the vampire.

The vampire was almost upon Jack and it seemed to Ben, looking on, that Mr Brown must inevitably fall on to the thorns. But the butler saw the danger at the last second and did the only thing he could to save himself – he shape-shifted into bat form and veered sharply away from Jack, up into the shadows of the palm trees.

Jack realized he was holding his breath. He let it out in a huge sigh of relief.

"That was too close for comfort," Ben said, and Jack nodded fervently in agreement. "Now let's find Emily and the professor and try to get out of here," Ben suggested. "Em! Emily! Where are you?" he called.

There was no answer. Ben drew breath to shout for her again, but Jack put a finger to his lips. "They ain't saying where they are," he whispered to Ben. "Mr Brown might get to them first."

Ben took the blood rose stem and held it up like a sword in front of him. "Stay close to me, Jack," he said, grimly. "We'll find them together."

Slowly, the boys moved down the aisle, straining their eyes to peer into the gloom. The palm trees – so graceful and elegant by daylight – seemed sinister and threatening in the gathering dusk. Any one of them could hide their foe. Many could easily shelter a fully grown man, let alone something the size of a bat.

"Professor, if you can hear me," Ben called, "we have the rose. Wait wherever you are and we'll come and find you."

They were almost at the far end of the Palm House when Jack's cap was swept off his head by some low-hanging palm leaves. He bent quickly to retrieve it and as he straightened up again, he glanced into the shadows of the shrubbery.

Two red eyes gazed back.

Jack yelled as the bat flew at him. The vampire was already changing shape into a man again and he caught both boys, and dragged them to the ground. Jack landed with a thump which knocked all the breath out of him. Ben tried to scratch Mr Brown with the blood rose, but the butler quickly caught his wrist in a powerful grip and squeezed. Ben cried out in pain and tried to fight, but he couldn't compete with the vampire's inhuman strength. In spite of his best efforts, his fingers loosened on the blood rose.

"Drop it," the vampire growled, "or I will snap your arm off here and now." He needn't have bothered to threaten. Ben's hand was completely numb and the rose fell from his grasp.

Mr Brown wrapped one arm around Ben and lifted him, struggling and kicking, off the floor. He hurled the boy away from him across the Palm House and then turned his attention to Jack.

Jack was crawling across the floor towards the blood rose, but before he could reach it Mr Brown grabbed him by the shoulder and dragged him to his feet. Jack felt the vampire's other hand grasp his hair and pull his head back so that his throat was bared. He peered up into Mr Brown's face. The butler was smiling and his fangs gleamed ominously as he bent his head to Jack's neck. Jack closed his eyes and listened to the pounding of his own heart as he waited for the vampire's bite.

The next thing Jack knew, he felt a sharp pain – but it was across his cheek, not in his neck as he had been expecting.

Mr Brown screamed and let go of Jack. Jack stumbled away from the vampire and then turned to see what had happened.

To his amazement he saw Emily slashing at the butler with the blood rose. Thin red weals opened on the vampire's face and he staggered back, clutching his head in his hands. He screamed again and fell on to the iron floor.

Jack watched in horrified fascination as cracks began to appear all over Mr Brown's skin. Then the cracks split open and Jack could see the butler's innards turning into a gritty grey powder that heaved and writhed. And then the powder consumed the vampire's entire body and he crumpled into a pile of ash. The clothes he had worn still lay there. Some of the ash trickled from his collar and the ends of his sleeves, and fell through the grating.

Ben picked himself up, feeling rather bruised and battered, and limped over to join Jack – and Emily, who was proudly brandishing the blood rose.

"What do you know?" she said. "It really *is* poisonous to vampires."

She seemed a touch unsteady on her feet. Her long hair was tangled and there was a trickle of blood on her forehead, but her smile was triumphant. Adensnap appeared and offered her his arm to lean on.

"My word!" he said, somewhat bemusedly. "My word!"

The little group of friends gathered around the remains of the vampire.

"We can do it, eh?" Jack said. "We really can fight vampires!" He put a finger to his scratched face and looked thoughtfully at the smear of blood there. *His* blood. It had never looked so precious to him as it did now.

"Yes. Yes, we can," Ben agreed proudly. He looked down at the professor, who had stooped to retrieve the keys to the Palm House from what was left of Mr Brown. "Now, let's go and make that potion, shall we, sir?" he asked.

The professor stood up with the keyring in his hand. "Yes, indeed!" he replied.

They made their way back to where the attendant's body lay by the door. His neck was broken, so badly that his head was almost looking over his shoulder. There was no point in checking to see if he was alive.

Emily looked away quickly. "The poor man," she breathed.

"At least he's properly dead," Ben said with brutal frankness. "It could be worse."

"We should. . ." Emily began.

". . .tell someone?" Ben asked. He shook his head regretfully. "I'm sorry, Em, but I don't think we can. You know what the police were like last time."

"He is right, my dear," Adensnap said sadly. "We should leave before someone finds us. It goes against the grain, but we can't afford to be locked up right now."

"But he was *murdered*," Emily protested.

Ben put an arm around her shoulders. "Yes, and you defeated his murderer," he pointed out. "That's justice – of a kind. Come on, Em. There's nothing more we can do." He took one last look down at the body. "No, actually, there is," he corrected himself. "We can make sure that this man is the last to die."

CHAPTER TWENTY-THREE

"Now!" shouted Jack, as the first rays of golden sunlight spilled over the horizon.

The professor tipped the crushed emerald leaves of the blood rose into the potion, which was steaming and simmering on the stove in the kitchen of his small Paddington home. At once a warm, sweet, rosy scent flooded the room.

All of them had been exhausted by the time they reached the professor's house the night before. Emily had wanted to send a message to Mrs Mills, letting her know that they were safe, but Ben was sure that Bedford Square was being watched, and they didn't dare send a message which might be intercepted by Sir Donald's servants.

Adensnap's housekeeper had attended to everyone's bumps and bruises, and then the professor had insisted that they try to get some sleep – sending Emily up to the guest room and letting Ben and Jack share a couch in the drawing room. In fact, excitement had kept them all awake and they were glad to start work on the potion when the clock struck four in the morning.

It was not the most convenient concoction to brew. The leaves of the blood rose had to be picked at sun*set* and added to the potion itself at sun*rise*. Emily and the professor had prepared and mixed the ingredients while Jack and Ben scanned the horizon from the kitchen window, eagerly awaiting the first glimpse of the sun, which the professor's almanac had informed them would rise at ten minutes to five that morning.

Emily examined the instructions that she and the professor had translated from the parchment. "Once the leaves have been added to the mixture, repeat the Renunciation of the Dark God, ten times, over the brew," she read aloud. "*U bah ti akot hasaw-chan. . .*" she began.

Jack was immediately struck by how strange and sinister the Ancient Mayan words sounded in the homely kitchen. By the time Emily had recited the full incantation ten times over, the atmosphere in the room was heavy with some weird, incomprehensible magic, and Jack felt strongly that something of great mystery and power had been created.

The professor gently took the pot from the stove and set it on the table. The friends crowded round to look. The surface shimmered gently in a haze of different shades of red. Some of the leaf fragments swirled idly on the surface before disappearing into the ruby depths.

"That will do it?" Jack asked dubiously.

"We followed the instructions to the letter, dear boy," Adensnap said. "The precise words, times of day, length of boiling, number of repetitions. We can't know whether it will work for sure, but at least we will have done our best."

Jack felt that that would be scant consolation if they failed, but kept the thought to himself.

The professor shooed them out of the kitchen and into the hallway, shutting the door behind them. He yawned and hid his mouth behind his hand. "Yes, a few more hours of sleep is what we all need. After you, dear girl."

With the professor bearing down upon her, Emily had no choice but to start up the stairs to the guest room. Adensnap followed, heading for his own bedroom. Ben and Jack glanced at each other in the doorway to the drawing room, then turned back to the stairs.

"Goodnight, Emily," Ben said very clearly. Adensnap didn't notice his somewhat measured tone. But Emily did, and she looked back.

Ben held up both hands, fingers splayed, and mouthed the words, *"Ten minutes."*

Emily nodded. "Goodnight, Benedict," she replied in a similar tone.

"Yes, yes, goodnight all," Adensnap said. His back was to the boys as he climbed the stairs and he hadn't noticed a thing. "Tell you what, we'll all be up at nine and the housekeeper will make us a smashing breakfast, eh?"

CHAPTER TWENTY-FOUR

Outside it was daylight. Inside, the closed curtains threw the professor's house into gloom. The old man's snores echoed down the stairwell.

Emily crept quietly down the stairs to join Ben and Jack in the hall. Then the three of them slipped into the kitchen and filled a small metal flask with the precious blood rose potion. Emily put it carefully into her bag, together with the ancient parchment that bore the vital incantation for the banishment ritual. Then she turned to the boys. "Are you sure we shouldn't tell the professor where we're going?" she asked them.

"He'll know where we've gone, Em," Ben reassured her. "It's better for us to slip out this way. He'd never let us go without him if he knew, and we can't let him face a horde of vampires. He'd never survive. . ."

"Goodness only knows whether *we'll* survive," Jack put in. "And we're much younger and fitter than the professor."

And on that grim note, Emily sighed and nodded, Ben opened the front door and the three friends stepped outside to face the day – and the vampire god, Camazotz.

An hour later the friends found themselves back in Mayfair.

The plan was clear. The parchment said the ritual had to be performed in one of Camazotz's places of power. They knew he spent his days in the cellar of Sir Donald Finlay's house. And they had seen what was down there – the box where he slept, the altar, the candles, the effigy, and even the corpses of his sacrificial victims. If the cellar wasn't a place of power, then nothing was. *And* they knew a way in.

So, Jack led Ben and Emily round the back way. It wasn't difficult to find the mews that ran behind Sir Donald's house. The backs of the houses loomed large above the stables, but the mews itself was sunny and cheerful in the daylight. Jack felt safe. He had kept his eyes open for strangers wrapped up against the sun, and seen none.

Finally they stood at the end of the alley between Sir Donald's house and its neighbour. They had fled down this gloomy brick passage two nights ago. The sun barely made its way past the high walls that ran its length and it did not look inviting.

"There's no one there," said Jack.

They could all see that there were no people – the

walls were too smooth and sheer to hide even a bat. And yet. . .

Ben swallowed. "Come on, then." He squared his shoulders and walked down the alley. Jack and Emily followed.

Now they were past the garden wall, and the bulk of the house towered over them. Ben had his eyes on the ground. "The coal chute was about here," he said. "Oh!"

He had found the spot where they had scrambled up from the cellar to escape the vampires. But the little hatch wasn't there any more. It had been neatly bricked up. The bricks looked fresh and new, set against their older, soot-blackened neighbours.

Ben stared at the spot where the hatch had been. "Blast," he whispered.

Emily slowly unshouldered her bag and opened it. "I was hoping we wouldn't need this," she said.

The boys craned their necks to peer inside. There was the flask of potion and the parchment. And beneath them lay the blood rose stem – minus the leaves that had been used to make the potion.

"You brought the blood rose!" Jack exclaimed.

Emily put the bag on the ground and knelt beside it. Then she took hold of the rose's stem – gingerly, to avoid the thorns – and carefully snapped it into three pieces.

"Perfect!" said Ben, as Emily handed a piece each to him and Jack. "Jack and I can fight our way in and. . ."

his voice died as he saw that Emily was keeping a piece for herself.

"Emily, you can't mean to—" he began again.

"I can," Emily interrupted flatly. Then she smiled fondly and pinched his cheek. "Oh, Ben. Do you honestly think I could wait outside? We're all in this together. You can complain after we've won."

Ben bit his lip and looked away. When he looked back there was steel in his gaze. "I'll be the one who confronts Sir Donald. I was there at the start. I want to end it."

Emily paused, then nodded. "Then you should take the potion and the parchment now," she told him. "There won't be time inside. And Jack and I will hold off the vampires for, well –" She faltered.

"For as long as it takes," Jack finished simply.

They walked out into the square, and squinted up at the front of the mansion. The windows stared vacantly back at them. The curtains were all drawn. Jack thought he saw one twitch, but he couldn't be sure.

They paused at the bottom of the steps, then walked on up to the front door, side by side. Before either of the others could stop him, Jack reached out and tugged on the bell-pull.

He shrugged at their amazed looks. "How else are we goin' to get in?" he asked.

They waited a long time.

"No one in?" suggested Ben, not really believing it.

"They might all be in the attic," Emily pointed out. So Jack rang the bell again, and again.

Eventually the door opened. A man stood inside the shadows of the house. Jack looked at the man's cap and scruffy coat, and thought he must be a builder. But then he noticed the pallor of his skin and the red gleam in his eyes, and realized that whatever he *had* been, he was now a vampire.

"What do you want?" the vampire asked.

"We have a message from Mr Brown," said Emily. "For the Master."

The vampire's eyes widened. "What message?" he demanded.

"This," said Jack. He brought his arm round from behind his back and slashed at the vampire with the sprig of blood rose that he clutched in his hand. The creature screeched and staggered back into the house. Jack, Ben and Emily ran in after it.

The vampire twisted and screamed on the floor. Its skin cracked and then split wide open – and where there should have been blood and living tissue, there was just a writhing mass of ash that finally fell in on itself and lay still.

Something hissed. Jack peered into the depths of the hallway and saw the dark shapes of vampires, crouching in the shadows, waiting. . .

He clutched his blood rose firmly and summoned all his courage. "Come on!" he shouted, and his cry echoed around the hallway. "Come on and fight!"

The vampires crept out of the shadows towards him.

Emily threw the front door open wide and sunshine splashed across the floor. The vampires jumped back. Before they realized what he was doing, Jack ran to the window on the right of the front door and dragged the curtains open. More sunbeams flooded the hall, and some of the vampires couldn't get out of the way fast enough. A sickening smell of burnt flesh filled the room.

A female vampire – young and well dressed – who had obviously been a wealthy lady once, was caught in the middle of the flood of sunshine. She screamed horribly and seemed to melt into her rich silk gown. Before Jack's eyes, the woman dissolved until she was nothing more than a heap of ash, surrounded by yards of lustrous blue silk.

Jack tore his gaze away and saw that Ben had swept back the curtains from the other window. Now a large patch of sunlight stretched across the hall. The friends had their battlefield and the vampires gathered around it, drawing closer and closer through the shadows.

There were so many of them that the vampires behind were pushing the others forward into the attack – and into the sunlight. Apparently they did not care that the sunbeams were destroying as many of their comrades as were Jack, Ben and Emily. They just kept pressing forward, oblivious to those dead and destroyed, their numbers seemingly endless.

Jack and Emily were intent on fighting the constant

stream of vampires. Emily shouted at Ben to make his way to the cellar, while she and Jack held the vampires back.

Ben looked over at the cellar door. It was on the sunlit side of the hall, but still there was a narrow strip of shadow all down that side of the room that the light from the window didn't quite reach. Ben glanced across at his sister and his friend. He caught Jack's eye briefly. Jack nodded to him and then returned to face the vampire onslaught. Ben ran for the cellar.

As he did so, several vampires noticed and ran to intercept, but Ben had a head start and he reached the door first. He turned the handle. For a moment he had the dreadful thought that Sir Donald might have locked the door from the inside – but the door swung open easily and Ben flung himself through it and into the darkness beyond.

At the bottom of the steps, Ben slowed. Everything seemed to be as he remembered it, except that there were fewer candles alight, so the room was dimmer than before. The smell of damp and the smell of blood were rank in his nostrils.

He turned to face the blood-soaked altar across the room. The golden bat and the golden crown were still there. The loathsome effigy of Camazotz still dominated the altar, and Ben felt that its gaze was, if anything, more malevolent than the last time he had seen it. He shivered and looked away.

His eyes fell on the long wooden box next to the altar. In there, in those few square feet, lay the most evil creature on earth, and Ben knew that he alone had the means to stop it.

He pulled the flask of potion out of his pocket and unscrewed the lid. Then he withdrew the parchment. Above, he could hear the battle raging. And with relief he noted that all the screams came from vampires.

Ben took a deep breath. Then, potion in one hand, parchment in the other, he approached the box.

He could see no kind of latch or handle, but the lid was loose. Tucking the parchment under his arm, he closed his fingers around the rim and threw the lid back. Then he grabbed the parchment again, ready to read the incantation.

But what he saw inside the box brought him up short. For there was nothing, no sign of Sir Donald. The box was empty.

"No!" he shouted in frustration. *"No, it can't be!"*

"Oh-h-h, ye-s-s-s." Ben clearly heard the reply. The very air around him seemed to whisper in mockery.

Ben whipped round, trying to see who – or *what* – had spoken.

As he turned, Sir Donald emerged from the shadows on the far side of the altar, and his eyes glinted red in the candlelight.

CHAPTER TWENTY-FIVE

"*So,*" intoned Sir Donald. And it was as if Ben heard two voices. One was Sir Donald's usual tones – though cold and distant, not warm as they had been when he was alive. The other seemed to emanate from the very air in the room. It was a sinister, deep vibration that could not have come from a human throat, and Ben *felt* rather than heard the words.

"*You have the blood rose potion. An intoxicating liquor for a boy,*" Sir Donald continued.

"I think I can cope," said Ben defiantly. "Can you?" And he ran at Sir Donald, raising his hand to fling the potion over the vampire god.

"*Stop!*" the god thundered.

And without intending to, Ben did. Some sort of force surrounded him like thick treacle, bogging him down, denying him movement. Ben found himself rooted to the spot, still clutching the flask and the parchment in his hands, but unable to use them.

Sir Donald approached and studied the parchment. *"The potion* and *the ritual!"* he said. *"You have been busy."* He gave a low, throaty chuckle. *"Once before was the Ritual of the Blood Rose used against me. It took the armies of Chac a day and a night even to come close. My servants fought against them, tooth and claw. And you come against me thus – two boys and a girl!*

"You have underestimated the strength of my servants. You see, they have no will but my own. They have no lives to protect for they are already dead. There is no sacrifice they are unwilling to make for me. How can you think you will prevail?"

He studied Ben a moment longer. *"It is good that Brown failed in his task. You are clearly stronger and will make a good servant. But before I change you, your mortal self will know my gift of despair."*

Sir Donald pointed at the parchment, still clutched in Ben's hand. The edges began to blacken and curl. It gave off a wisp of smoke, then burst into flames. Ben stared at it in horror as his skin began to burn. The pain was indescribable, but he could not move to help himself. He watched in anguish as the words of the incantation were consumed.

"And now," Sir Donald commanded, *"pour away the potion."*

Against his will, Ben felt his wrist begin to turn.

Jack and Emily stood in the alcove of the cellar door,

fighting back the countless vampires that came at them. One by one, the vampires were destroyed by the lethal thorns of the blood rose, but there were always others to take their places. And, with their savage claws, the vampires were managing to inflict some nasty injuries on Jack and Emily before they dissolved into ash.

There was a deep, red gash across Jack's face and a long, bleeding weal around Emily's neck. Fighting with the blood rose was a two-edged sword, because the vicious thorns scratched vampires and humans indiscriminately. The friends' hands were covered in blood and scratches.

Suddenly, the vampires started to back away.

Emily looked around in confusion. "W-where are they going?" she gasped.

Jack was watching the retreating vampires warily. "I dunno. . ." he said. And then he yelled and ducked as a vampire bat flew at him. He lunged up at it with the blood rose, and felt it connect. The bat veered away and crumbled into ash.

The vampires appeared to have given up attacking in their human forms in favour of this new assault. The bats came swiftly, straight across the hall – through the sunlight. They smouldered a little where the sunbeams fell on them, but they flew so quickly, and were so agile, that their teeth and claws could inflict a powerful wound in that time.

One bat, then another, then what seemed like the

entire swarm, clustered around Jack and Emily. Jack staggered back against the onslaught, flailing wildly with the blood rose. But he was hopelessly outnumbered. The bats forced him back into the shadows, where someone hit him hard over the head.

Jack fell to the ground in a daze. A booted foot kicked the blood rose out of his grasp and powerful hands hauled him to his feet. Fingers like steel gripped his head and a sturdy arm was wrapped around his neck.

Emily had jumped into the middle of the sunlight in an attempt to escape the bats, now she stared at Jack in dismay.

"Surrender," shouted a harsh voice, "or I will break the boy's neck."

"Don't—" Jack croaked. The arm tightened around his neck and choked him off. He stared mutely at Emily, hoping that she would never surrender, hoping that the vampire holding him would kill him, there and then – he didn't want to live in a world where he and his friends had failed.

But Emily's eyes filled with tears of frustration, and she let the blood rose drop to the floor. One vampire kicked the front door closed, others pulled the curtains shut and the hall was cast back into darkness. Strong hands took hold of Emily from behind and she heard a voice say, "We will bring them to the Master."

CHAPTER TWENTY-SIX

Ben did not notice that the noise above had stopped, because he was entirely lost in the tremendous effort required to fight the will of Camazotz. The demon god's mind was inside his own – an invisible force focused on controlling his body, focused on making his hand tip the flask further and further. . .

"Ben!" cried Emily.

Ben glanced up in shock and saw Emily and Jack standing at the foot of the cellar stairs, vampires on either side of them. The distraction broke his concentration and the flask tipped, spilling half of its precious contents. He was standing by the altar, where the stone slabs of the floor had been torn up to make that vile stone table, and the potion soaked away into the bare earth. Immediately Ben doubled his resolve against Camazotz, but it was too late. He felt himself tip the flask again. A drop fell from the rim, then another, and another and then the rest of the rosy potion splashed on to the ground.

At once the invisible bonds holding Ben snapped. He staggered back, staring horrified at the damp patch of earth. There was a faint smell of roses in the air, and a couple of bubbles where the wasted potion had been, but that was all.

Dark laughter filled the cellar – the inhuman, echoing laughter of Camazotz. His human voice had gone completely. All that was left were the hideously triumphant tones of the Mayan vampire god.

"And so it ends!" he said. *"Come close, children. Come close and kneel before me. Join the ranks of my servants and you will be privileged to see me in my true form."*

Ben felt the invisible force take hold of him again, compelling him to step forward. Emily was moving towards Sir Donald too, though Ben could see she was straining back.

And Jack surprised everyone. Sir Donald was only expecting resistance. He wasn't expecting anyone to run towards him of their own volition. But Jack darted forward and scooped up a handful of the damp, potion-soaked earth. "Say it!" he shouted. "Say the words!" And he hurled the earth at Sir Donald.

The vampire god roared with fury and back-handed Jack across the cellar.

"I can't," Ben moaned. "Sir Donald burnt the parch—"

But Emily was speaking. She had helped to translate

220

the incantation, she had recited it over the potion while it was brewing, and she had memorized the words. *"U bah ti akot hasaw-chan,"* she cried.

As Emily spoke, the potion-soaked earth clinging to Sir Donald's face seemed to burn itself into his skin. Sir Donald roared again and the vampires screamed in eerie unison. For the second time, Ben felt himself freed from Camazotz's grip. He flung himself to the floor, scooped up another handful of the damp earth and threw it over the demon god.

"Camazotz u hun katun!" said Emily.

Sir Donald howled in pain. He scrabbled at the earth on his face, trying to brush the scorching, searing soil away. But his strength was fading.

"Camazotz kin winal tun. . ."

And the vampires were wavering. As their Master weakened, so they too began to lose their powers. They could no longer control their forms. They seemed to shift between bats and ordinary humans.

"Chuwen keh tu bah ha atun!"

Sir Donald's scream became deafening. The friends crouched with their hands over their ears. Sir Donald's form was splitting, disintegrating. A blinding red flame burst out through cracks in his skin and his body slowly, slowly crumbled into ash. A cloud hung over the heap of ash, and, for just a moment, it formed a terrible face – the *true* face of Camazotz.

Jack got a fleeting impression of an ancient, evil,

twisted visage, with smouldering eyes that seemed to be endless chasms into the depths of a hell, old beyond all imagining.

Jack felt himself falling as he gazed into those eyes, but then the face was gone and a large bat formed in its place. The bat flew around the cellar, screeching in rage. Then it swooped down to the altar and grabbed the golden bat and the golden crown in its claws.

With a rumble, and the sound of rocks tearing apart, the floor of the cellar shuddered and began to split into a gaping abyss. The altar shook and the horrifying effigy of Camazotz crashed to the floor. As the chasm gaped wider, the altar teetered then plummeted into the depths.

Emily and Jack jumped back, but Ben swayed on the edge, arms flailing as he tried to balance. For a moment he had a clear view. The chasm plunged way, way, down, surely far beyond the limits of the planet. Smoke, fire and lava churned and bubbled far below. For just a moment, before Jack grabbed him and pulled him to safety, Ben realized he was staring into a pit of Hell.

Camazotz flew unhesitatingly into the yawning pit, still clutching his golden treasures. He was followed a moment later by the vampires in the cellar. They had settled on their bat forms and they swooped after their Master. There was a pause, and then more bats burst through the door from the house above. They swept towards the friends like black river rapids, and the three ducked to let the bats fly over them. The creatures plunged down into Hell after their god, and with a mighty boom the chasm slammed shut again.

And then there was silence. A silence so heavy and total it overwhelmed the senses.

Jack, Emily and Ben looked at one another. Nobody spoke. They were all feeling a profound sense of relief that somehow their plan had worked. Camazotz and his vampire plague had seemingly been banished to Hell itself.

The friends turned and trudged, silent and weary, back up the cellar stairs. Jack was the last to leave the room. As he was about to pass through the door, he turned and took one last look back at the cellar below. The hideous effigy of Camazotz caught his eye. For a moment he fancied it was staring at him – not looking in his direction with the fixed gaze of a statue, but really glaring at him, through eyes filled with hate.

As Jack stared back, mesmerized, the statue's eyes glowed red in the gloom. And suddenly Jack heard a voice. It was the voice of Camazotz, not booming and echoing from the air around him, but vibrating inside his head, as if the demon god was speaking only to him.

This is not the end. Live in fear, for I shall return – and then, you will know what it means to have angered a GOD!

The red glow in the statue's eyes faded. With a shudder, Jack tore himself away and ran to warn Ben and Emily.

CHAPTER TWENTY-SEVEN

Jack caught up with his friends in the hallway. "It ain't over!" he cried. "I heard 'im speaking just now. And 'e hasn't gone for good."

"Well, no," Ben agreed. "But one thousand years is a very long time, Jack. I think it will do for now." He turned towards the front door.

"No, no, you don't understand," Jack went on urgently, the words tumbling out of his mouth in his eagerness to explain. "The ritual didn't work properly or something. And Camazotz is going to return – sooner than we think. I heard 'is voice in my head. And the statue – its eyes, they went red and, and. . ."

"Calm down, Jack," soothed Emily gently. "You're just overwrought. We saw Camazotz fly down into the pit. I don't think he's coming back."

"But—" Jack tried again.

"Emily's right, Jack," Ben broke in comfortingly. "We've all been through a pretty terrifying experience.

225

Your mind's playing tricks on you, that's all."

Jack sighed. Part of him wanted to believe they were right – that the stress had got to him, that he had imagined that last evil promise from the vampire god. But deep down he knew he hadn't imagined it at all. Camazotz might have gone, but Jack felt sure that the banishment was only a temporary solution.

Still, he realized, there was no point in trying to convince his friends at the moment. And with a shake of his head, he followed them out of the house.

In a long coat and a battered top hat, Professor Adensnap was sitting on the balustrade outside the front door. He rose to his feet as Jack, Ben and Emily came down the steps. He pushed up the brim of his hat with his umbrella and beamed at them. His glasses slipped off his nose. "From the fact that you're walking about in daylight, and leaving of your own volition, I presume you succeeded!" he said cheerfully.

"How did you know we were here?" asked Emily.

"My dear girl, where else would you be?" Adensnap replied. "Thought you'd leave me out of the fun, eh, what?"

"Professor," began Ben. "Honestly, we didn't—"

Adensnap waved him into silence. "I know, I know, dear boy. I'd have done the same in your place." He put one arm around Ben's shoulders, the other around Jack. "I'm immensely proud of you all."

"Ben's hurt," Emily told him.

Ben looked down at his burnt hand in surprise. For a moment, he had actually forgotten, but the skin was blackened with red, weeping cracks across his palm.

"Eh? Oh my." The professor took Ben's hand gently and pulled back the sleeve. "Can you move your fingers?" Ben could, though he winced when he did. "Very good." Adensnap whipped off his scarf and used it to make a sling. "We'll put some ice on it and get it cleaned and looked at. It's a noble wound, young Cole. A noble wound."

"It doesn't feel noble," muttered Ben. "It just hurts."

"Well, I think it's time you young people went home, now that all this is over," said the professor. "Shall I hail a cab, eh?"

Ben and Emily agreed enthusiastically, but Jack fell suddenly silent. He was thinking about his friends, about all they had been through together and about how it had felt to be – almost – part of a family. Now that "all this" was over, as the professor said, he supposed all the rest was over, too. It was time for him to go home – home to the docks – and even though a part of him looked forward to seeing his old haunts again, he realized that a greater part of him did not want to say goodbye to his new family.

Jack sighed and looked up to see Emily watching him.

She smiled and laid a hand on his arm, and – almost as if she knew what he'd been thinking – she said, "You *are* intending to stay with us, aren't you, Jack? Ben and I were hoping that Bedford Square could be home to all of us from now on. . ."

Jack looked at her in doubtful amazement – not quite sure he could believe his ears. But then Ben walked over and slapped him on the back.

"Come on, Jack," Ben said. "It wouldn't be the same without you."

And Jack knew it was true and found himself too full of emotion to speak. He nodded instead and gave Emily a smile. And Professor Adensnap patted him kindly on the shoulder and quietly drew aside to flag down a cab.

A four-wheeler soon came along and Jack, Ben and Emily all piled in with the professor.

"Bedford Square, please," said Ben, and the cab rattled off as Ben and Emily started telling Professor Adensnap all about the battle with Camazotz.

When they had finished giving their account, Jack added what he had seen and heard before he left the cellar.

"A chilling warning, indeed, my young friend. But probably just the work of your overanxious imagination," responded the professor cheerfully, as the cab drew up outside the house in Bedford Square. "A good meal and a good rest are what you need now, I think."

And that was that.

Jack climbed down from the four-wheeler, still far

from convinced that Camazotz's words had been the product of his own imagination. On the other hand, he had to acknowledge that he had been tired and anxious – perhaps his friends and the professor were right. He certainly hoped so.

"Come on, Jack!" called Emily.

Jack blinked and realized that he had been lost in thought. The others were all waiting for him at the top of the steps to the house. Ben gave him a reassuring smile, and Jack decided to put his worries about Camazotz out of his mind. He grinned at his friend, and ran up the steps of his new home.

EPILOGUE

"Checkmate, by George!" the professor exclaimed. "That's one each. How about another game to decide the winner?"

"You're on," Ben laughed. The two of them began to set out the pieces for the re-match. Ben's hand was neatly bandaged so the professor did most of the work.

Professor Adensnap had joined the three friends in a celebratory evening meal. Now Jack and Emily were watching him and Ben play chess, and offering encouragement from the sidelines.

Jack felt a happy sense of warmth and belonging. His mind drifted back to his old life, a hard life, eked out at the docks where he had first met Ben. With a sigh he got up and wandered over to the window. He slid behind the curtains and gazed out over London towards his old home.

Suddenly his eyes were drawn to a black shape wheeling across the sky. For a moment it was clearly outlined against the moon – the sinister, unmistakeable shape of a large black bat – then it was gone, disappearing into the distance, heading east.

Jack shivered and wondered whether it could have been Camazotz in his bat form. It had certainly looked too big to be an ordinary bat. He felt an eerie certainty that the fight against the vampire god was far from over. But he knew that no amount of persuasion from him was going to convince Ben and Emily. Well, he thought grimly, they had defeated Camazotz once. If the Mayan god did return, at least he, Jack, would be ready.

He moved away from the window and went back to join the party.

VAMPIRE
Plagues

PARIS

*Strong hands grasped Jack's shoulders painfully from
behind, and he looked up into the eyes of a vampire.
He felt the claws prick through his skin, and small flowers
of blood welled up through the white cloth. The vampire
growled, and Jack felt the fangs sink into his throat...*

Jack wants to believe it was only a dream –
the vampires are gone. Banished for a thousand
years by an ancient ritual that sent their leader to
the depths of Hell. But he isn't so sure. That voice
still echoes in his mind, the voice of the vampire god,
promising to return. Jack's friends Ben and Emily
say it's just his imagination, but it seemed so real.

Maybe Victorian London is safe – but a strange
sickness is raging in Paris. A familiar sickness, that
leaves its victims drained of blood. It seems the vampires
have moved on, and the fight must follow them...

Catch VAMPIRE PLAGUES –
the series will be with you for life...